THE KOR

WARREN FAHY

ISBN 978-1-63789-576-4
Gordian Knot is an imprint of Crossroad Press Publishing

For information address Crossroad Press at 141 Brayden Dr., Hertford, NC 27944
www.crossroadpress.com

Cover art and design by Michael Limber
Illustrations by Kyushik Shin

First Crossroad Press Edition

*

Little Erg climbed the granite spire, chasing the sun's tail. Nowhere in the world did the sun remain except here, moving over this rock that pierced the emerald sky. The sun vanished even as his feet touched the still-warm peak. He shouted as he jumped into the air and the last ray set his fur on fire as he glimpsed the sun's rim below the eastern edge of the world.

When his feet touched the stone it was already cool. Erg wet his black fingers on his pink tongue and smoothed the chocolate fur to each side beneath his obsidian eyes. He had climbed the Cinter, just as he told them. Clapping his hands once in triumph, he surveyed the fading landscape of Tai-Raynee as torches dotted the fields and stars pierced the turquoise sky.

Sitting perfectly still with arms folded on the granite pinnacle, only the kor child could see the strange glow gathering beyond the southern horizon. He guessed that it was a fire on the side of the world kors never saw. Like a chunk of melting gold, it rose, burning the sky instead of the land. "*Aaah!*" he cried, pawing the air. Like a leaping ghost, the fire emerged and it moved across the sky, dragging an arching wake behind it, before it sank behind the horizon only minutes after it had appeared.

The bot child leaped down the sheer pinnacle in the starlight from ledge to ledge, shouting at the kors below to warn them. But they were too far below to hear him.

When he finally reached the roots of the Cinter, he ran as fast as he could into the cave.

In the cave the light was dim, delirious. Incense burned in a circle of niches carved high in the back wall, a ring of red coals around the 9,000-year-old prophet Sor, the First, who gazed down at 22 disciples.

The 22 "sors" who resided in the cave made Truth for the *Koroshi*. On the walls around them, the shapes of the Immurtai world were painted: curled ferns, green parrots with blue and yellow eggs, flying red hordes of many-legged things, the "giss" roots of all shapes and colors, tastes and textures. And the pearl-white fishes, the red elks, the orange butterflies, the yellow lilies, the kors. All these images had faded as daylight drained through the cave's mouth. Only the fresco on the ceiling was now visible, an eruption of phosphorescent stones showing the creation and the apocalypse, each being one and the same brief lie before the Infinite Truth.

The sor Ez admired the skull of Holy Sor and chased the answers in his dark eyes with muted questions. He was never able to follow them deep enough, and he was humbled—such things took patience. Not the patience of one kor, but of all the *Koroshi*, together through time. At any moment along the way kors could not see Truth, but only imitate it, grace it, strive not to offend it with their own falseness.

Ez's body was withered, his right thumb missing. Streaks of white fur curved from the inner corners of his ash-gray eyes down the hollows of his cheeks. His lips pressed into a horizontal line divorced from frown or smile as he smelled the pungent smoke of green manthril flowers, rising in straight lines around Sor in the perfect silence.

That was when the tiny kor child burst in on thrashing little legs, waving his arms and shouting, "A star is dying!"

The sors gasped and lifted their arms as the boy's feet slung a colonnade of layered ash and dust behind him.

When the child saw their faces he was frightened. But when he turned back, the sors' tall, muscular attendant, Tor, caught him, and brought him, struggling, to the sors. Tor bowed then and then he left the cave.

The boy was held down until peace was restored and the stillness returned and the Truth was forgiven. But the boy shocked them with one last whisper: "My ghost will rise, as big as Forever."

The sors sat in a circle, silent for a long measure afterwards. Then Ez recited the words of Sor: "The shout lasts no longer on the air than the whisper."

The sor On, who was all white, sighed at Ez's stubborn need to state the Truth, which was only made less true when uttered by lips.

Not a word was spoken as they used their left hands, working long into the night like a natural process, like time or decomposition. And when they were finished, the wind sighed around the mighty Cinter outside the cave and a few more grains of granite blew from its shoulders onto the fields. They had proven their devotion to the Truth before the lies of the dawn stirred the world, once again.

I

Dawn shattered the night into the day's infinite shapes and colors. The ageless industries of the kors sprang to life around the Cinter.

In the forest by the River Eri in the Fishers province, a little kor with obsidian eyes sat atop a tree with his little arms folded. He smelled the wood smoke scenting the forest and heard the others chopping branches and chipping stones as they went about the day's first chores. The morning mist burned off in the green sky.

"Erg, get down from there!" Sannava yelled.

Erg pointed from the top of the tree at a smaller tree.

His other sister, Azurel, hid her eyes. "Erg, don't!"

"Here I GO!" Erg squealed, and he sprang into the sky. As the dawn lit his fur, he nearly passed the slender top branch of the smaller tree and plunged to the ground, but he snatched a supple bough at the last moment and it tipped and flung back. Little Erg twirled around like a rag toy, laughing until the tree was still. Then he zigzagged down the branches to the ground and bounded onto Azurel's head.

He folded his little arms and glared at Sannava, sticking his pink tongue out. His sisters laughed wearily and Erg clapped his hands.

"Little Erg, you stop doing that," Sannava scolded. "If you keep climbing higher every time you jump, you'll break yourself into bits." She wagged a finger at him as Azurel giggled. "Stop encouraging him, Azzy."

Little Erg

Erg cocked his furry head and grinned slyly. Sannava poked at him and he leaped off Azurel's head, and it seemed he had vanished. Then, even as Sannava and Azurel spotted him on top of the small tree, he catapulted to the top of the bigger tree.

For a moment only the sound of tools dropping on the ground could be heard. Little Erg swung on the bending treetop as though he had done nothing remarkable, yet the kors who had witnessed it were dumbstruck by Erg's feat. He appeared to dance upside-down on the tip of the tree, rolling capriciously in the leaves as he caught the first ray of the dawning sun, as though the sky was his home.

Kors eventually went back to their business, but the child's prowess would soon be famous throughout Tai-Raynee.

"Sannava, Erg is wild!" Azurel said, with delight. A svelte, sandy-furred kiori, her bright blue eyes glittered with dark excitement as she watched her little brother.

Her sister Sannava had sky-green eyes and an athletic body covered by gold fur that lay in elegant patterns. She looked wryly at Azurel. "It's frightening almost, isn't it, Azzy?"

"He's different from other boys and girls," Azurel said. "He's more kor than the rest of us, I think."

"Oh, Azzy, you better become an Artist or everyone will call you mad."

Azurel had recently completed carving a statue of her sister Sannava in hopes of persuading the sors to let her become an Artist. She was one of those kors who made up words, a vocation quietly honored by Hunters even though it was a risky business. Some of Azurel's words had caught on, to Sannava's surprise. She had recently heard a farmer use one of them: "dain," it was. Those who used that strange word were all very good kors, strong and memorable. It meant something good, she knew. It had something to do with mixing a kor's *Demurtai* with the Immurtai and the Immurtai with the *Demurtai,* a religious idea of some kind, and probably blasphemous. But

Azurel said everyone did it, even the sors, before she ever made up her word.

Sannava raised her hand to shield the sun as she looked at Erg. "I'll take Erg home."

"I'm going to the crafting place," sighed Azurel, her blue eyes wandering.

"Bye," Sannava said. "Don't get lost."

Little Erg giggled, tussling with the branches as bristling shafts of dawn caressed him. He looked at the tower of stone in the distance. "Tonight!" he whispered.

Azurel saw him point his tiny finger at the Cinter.

At the same moment, far away, the Hunt was about to begin.

Twelve hands tall and four wide at the shoulder, Win was a mighty kor, even at 40. There was a quiet admiration among the Hunters for Win, whose short brown fur was tufted thick with a diamond of gray fur centered on his chest. Win was one of what the Hunters called the Wanto Warre, the "Furious Four." He stood at the edge of a green meadow frosted with red and yellow flowers, assessing the game in the valley below.

Zen, who was also known as Mimu or "Papa," bent his 400 pounds over the youngsters, his own sons and Win's listening closely to his instruction as he explained the elaborate tradition. Most of the young hunters were kioros, male kors, but there were kioris who had chosen to be hunters, as well, and all had spent the day before preparing for this stage of the hunt. Wooden pegs had been driven two arms apart into the soft grassland of the valley below. Between these posts were strung bolas. Two strings of the three-stringed bolas were fitted into grooves at the top of the posts about four hands above the ground, hidden in the waving grass. The strings and posts had been stained green by Hearthkeepers and Hunter children with grass juice. A field 60-arms-long and 20 wide had been set. This place, the Valley of the Chomp, had been the arena of countless performances like the one that was about to commence.

The Hunter Zen

Zen joined Win as they looked at the herd moving down the valley: fat spring antelopes with red stripes on their white bellies and tall ears on their graceful heads. Their red, fluted horns were the symbol scored into all the earthenware of the kor kitchen. The animals grazed nimbly and tentatively in the valley like a school of minnows between river reeds. The hunters grinned, for they knew they had a prize herd—one which could yield more food and skins than any other this month.

A few tumbleweeds, common on the savanna, rolled down the valley from about a mile away on the left side. They had been released in the direction of the wind through the herd, one by one, by a hidden group of hunters.

"I'll go," Win said.

Zen nodded, as he was the older of the two and had done it a few more times than Win. The kors rolled a basket in the shape of a large drum to the edge of the valley with a camouflage of brambles lashed over its surface.

The kors pulled bunches of grass from the field and rubbed it into Win's fur. The grass, laden with spring pollen, would hide him from the sensitive noses of the antelopes. The drum-basket was unfastened and he bent inside it as Zen fastened the bramble flap.

Gripping the handles of antelope horn inside the basket, Win rolled it forward, heading to the right of the herd with the grass's slant. He kept the speed slow and lazy, catching his bearings each time he rose upright, pausing when the wind paused. Twenty minutes passed before he rolled next to the large bragging-horned buck at the herd's flank. Three perfectly timed tumbleweeds rolled past him, sent by kors concealed on the ridge upwind.

The stag antelope pinned one of the decoys under its front hoof and began nibbling at the soft sprigs on the ends of the twigs. It lifted its proud head, grinding its mouth as Win approached. It stopped chewing and one nostril flared in Win's direction. Its long ears twitched. The wind shifted and bent the grass toward Win; the animal stooped and grabbed another mouthful.

Without pausing, Win steered the drum-basket so that some of its protruding twigs actually brushed the hind leg of the stag, and then passed on about an arm's length to its other side. Bursting from the flap in the drum, perfectly positioned, Win mounted the convulsing beast. Grabbing its horns, he pounded his heels with rib-breaking ferocity into its sides and roared at the herd before him.

The herd surged up the valley. Win's mount *clicked* and cried, charging behind. Wrenching its horns, Win zigzagged the frantic beast behind the others, steering them toward the bola field.

Other hunters in their troop now rose from the tall grass and shouted, swinging clubs and funneling the game between them. The herd struck the bola field, their long legs tangling and breaking amid the whistling lines and thudding stones. In the chaos, antelopes leaped one over another, goring each other, struggling toward the top of the rising heap.

The hunters closed in and speared the vulnerable prey in a double phalanx. Seventy antelope, and two red elk, were taken from a herd of 200 that day, with no deaths of kors, and one injury only.

Win drove his flint knife into the nerve under the neck ridge of his mount, and the animal slowed down, first galloping, then walking, then falling dead in five heartbeats as Win jumped from its back, completing the ancient ritual.

This was the traditional method of hunting, executed to perfection. It was also a method meant for bounteous spring days like this one. It was an art form, often observed by the sors. It was the Way to Hunt, and the sors did not sanction any other way.

In harder times, however, when Hunters were forced to go farther afield for game, each troop relied on kors like Win and Zen for what they called the "Other Ways." It was for this reason that each hunter in Win's and Zen's troop carried flint for driving herds with brush fires, axes for digging pits and carving spikes, and lengths of cured leather cords to string between trees, alongside ritual bolas.

The average hunting troop comprised 50 or 60 kors. Scouts fanned ahead, traveling alone for stealth. Two lines of kors, called wings, dropped back in a 'V' behind the scouts. The leaders of the troop traveled at the point of the V and used a lexicon of animal noises to communicate along the wings.

When the kors combed the forest many animals never knew it. The hunters avoided alerting any game until they found a large enough group to encircle and attack. Then the forest rocked and shrieked as the beasts and birds flew into panic.

Though troops were not supposed to compete, when unmonitored on the "Far Fields," they committed many sacrileges in order to outdo each other. Each troop had become expert at avoiding the ceremonial Way to Hunt, and each troop had become fastidious at concealing their tactics from rivals.

Other troops sometimes caught Zen and Win in the midst of a bountiful harvest beside a fire-blackened field. "How have you managed such a wondrous hunt, Mimu?" they would ask, seeing that firebreaks had been cleared in advance. "There were mishaps that caused great blazes to our good fortune," Zen would respond, grinning brashly as the youngsters behind him giggled.

Many "accidents" happened in Zen's and Win's troop: great pits opened in the ground or whole herds plunged off cliffs. Yet hunters never discussed anything but the Way to Hunt when home from the Far Fields, and they never, absolutely never, gave another troop away. This was the unwritten code of the Hunters, who had fed the *Koroshi* well for many centuries.

Great hunters were celebrated by the kors. Their business was a sport and a spectacle to the rest of the tribe. Kors would gather on fine days like this one, far enough away not to be a nuisance, so they could watch the precise drama of the Hunt in the Valley of the Chomp. The sors, for their part, called the Hunters' the noblest of occupations, though for reasons none of the Hunters would ever understand.

The troop brought their trophies on travois up the gentle valley to the southwestern edge of Tai-Raynee and when they reached the community tannery, they were greeted by running kor boys and girls and beaming, proud kioris. They skinned the animals and hung the hides on leather cables for the Tanners and the younger kors to cure. The hunters drained the blood and butchered their game, separating the various meats into large baskets lined with broad leaves. Kors arrived with giss and other goods to trade and carried meat on travois back to homes throughout Tai-Raynee. Some meats were hung out to be cured, smoked and dried, an occupation of the Tanners, most of whom were kioris, though kioros, too, could be Tanners if they chose it.

Zen, Win, and Rueez, a younger, fiery hunter, if smaller than the other two, worked especially fast on the haul, each with their own techniques. Tanners clamored over their hides so clean did they leave them. Zen threw the last cut into a basket and clamped down the lid as the wind flowed over the luminous plain. "Best haul and the first done, too," he said as he bit into an onion. He was 50-years-old and stood 11-hands-tall, with broad chest and a head covered with thick cinnamon hair. A jet-black and snow-white beard swirled on his jaw and rugged patterns of chestnut fur radiated over the furrows of his face. He had blue eyes in that gregarious face, white teeth, and a straight and clever black nose. A swirl of white fur pinwheeled on his chest like a galaxy that could be seen in the winter sky. The wind ruffled Zen's fur. "Ah, wind, blow!" he yelled, and nearby children giggled. "This is good. Eh, Win?"

He banged his chest and breathed in, his black lips curving back over his cunning teeth.

Win smiled and nodded at his friend.

The kioris brought out pails of river water, laughing as they splashed them over the victorious hunters, washing away the blood and sweat. Zen shivered ridiculously, making the girls laugh louder and recoil.

It was the Fifth Day, and there would be feasts all over Tai-Raynee tonight. It was spring, and it was warm, and there was bounty.

Zen lifted the basket of fresh meat and gave it to Win. "Take that home to Sara quick and get over to my house. There's much juice waiting, and much work, too. We'll get in as much as possible before the sun goes and eat at your house after."

"I'm going for wood," Rueez said.

"How much wood can a little kor like Rueez haul?" Win jested.

"You'd be surprised, deadweight!" Rueez replied. Win swung an arm at the smaller Rueez, who dodged it, laughing. "I'm too fast for you," he said from a distance. "I am the bird, and you are the dirt!" He danced and laughed.

"Then fly away and bring us your twigs," Win growled. "But we're not building a nest!"

Rueez turned toward the river in the distance as he headed for the forest on its banks. "I'll see *you* at Zen's!"

Zen was building an addition onto his house, a thing he had wanted to do since he was a young kor. It would be a "feast hall," where all his many friends could celebrate hunts, and have tales, and sing, and dance. And all his many friends were helping to raise Zen's dream: a feast hall with a long table and benches and a place for a fire and horns on the beams and walls and Zen and all his friends and family and fellow hunters could gather there for boisterous revelry and good cheer on deep winter nights—that was the way Zen described his dream to them.

"I'll get this to Sara right away," Win said. "She's trying another way, cooking with the bark of red trees."

"*Hmm*, that should be interesting," Zen approved.

Then Win gathering up Tuton, his eldest son, and little Erg, his youngest son, who had been twirling about on the gables of the tannery's roof, and they made out across Tai-Raynee for home.

Sitting in a circle spaced apart on the grass around the base of the Cinter, the 22 sors were out, white and gray in the burning daylight. They greeted the cloying spread of clutter and clatter with stoic silence. The day's cacophony was a harsh duty for them. It was a heavy trial to preside over the endless chase of the "crackar" things.

It disturbed them to witness the green fields in the northern province of Tai-Raynee turned over red in the wind by the fall plows, and to see the smoke from the fires in the south where the Hunters' province was, and to hear the ceaseless bangs and whipsawing of the Crafters cracking their bones and braiding their leathers.

The Cinter was the trunk that supported the three branches of Tai-Raynee, a sharp, twisting tower of stone that had entered the sors' dreams, presiding over nine millennia of myth and memory. During the day, the sors sat cross-legged around the base of the Cinter, the green plain rising around it to the high northern horizon.

Brooding in the south side of the Cinter, the sors' cave peered down from a crag, a mound raised to its mouth. The land sloped steeply beneath the Cinter and only a small mound was raised on its northern side. Twenty-two giant stone blocks around the Cinter may have determined the sors' number in some ancient time. Each sor sat in front of one of these stone cubes and their forty-four eyes radiated over the kors.

Each morning, flat discs of baked red clay were placed beside the sors' left knees. Attendants spooned a black daub of river mud onto the plates. The sors drew circles and lines randomly in the fine mud throughout the day until it dried ash-white. In the afternoon, attendants collected the discs and baked them in kilns, later delivering them far out on the fields in countless rows that covered the plain north of Tai-Raynee. More than halfway up this steep plain, starting from the outskirts of the green farmland, the dull red pallets had been laid down over eons. This slope was called The Days, and it rose in banded colors of decomposing clay like the layers in a cliff, stretching for 50 miles, or 17 stins, ending in a thick band of green that reached higher than the Cinter and blended with the sky, ending in a cliff that was said to be three stins tall plunging into a green sea.

Attendants brought the courses of *Koroshi* resource to the sors each day. At dawn, they were served steaming giss soup that was made from the roots, which grew in all colors and flavors and textures and properties and were cultivated in the fashion of potatoes by the Farmers in the rainy season. The broth was flavored with seasonal herbs, berries, bean nuts, and spices of all three regions. At noon, the sors ate raw fish and crustaceans from the Fishers and drank bowls of cool river water tinged with leaf flavors. At dinner, they ate the largest meal; when the sun was gone and there was darkness. Each of them, according to ritual, ate roasted tongue, then testicle, then eye, then liver, then tripe, then flank, then marrow, then brain from the Hunters' prey, followed by a draught of fermented berry juice and mother's milk, before they retired into the cave.

On the Fifth Day, they fasted. At the end of the Fifth Day, sors met with their emissaries and attendants in the cave and then sent them away as they ate the black giss and drank the blood of a sloth and their minds started the long and arduous loop out from the cave between the stars and back again to the cave.

The place of the Crafters was nearest to the sors, encircling the Cinter, where they practiced the tradition-steeped conventions of manufacture. In silence they chipped the stone axes, knives and spearheads, and produced skin-craft and horn-craft from the Hunters' issue; they made baskets, bramble-decoys, fish-netting, spear shafts and woodcraft from the Farmers' and Gatherers' issue; they made fish-bone combs and brushes, shell-craft and earthenware from the Fishers' issue.

The Crafters traditionally worked facing inward, toward the sors. The sors did not defecate in the cave but in plain view of the Crafters, their shriveled posteriors aimed right at them. At first, young artisans giggled at this provocation, for they thought it was a funny mistake by doddering old fools. They soon learned it was not a mistake and not to suffer their giggles' consequences, and to simply not look. Some looked and it haunted them, and they became somber and strange, invisible to others. A few of the faithful anticipated, even revered the spectacle, as though it was a revelation of truth, and these held themselves to be above those who did not look.

As a rule, the Crafters toiling in the shadow of the Cinter were quieter than other kors, and there was a peculiar sort of emptiness in their eyes, whether affected or sincere, as they motioned the craft of ages before the wizened sors.

Outside the circle of the Crafters was the circle of guards, who were called "korensis." They protected the *Koroshi* and carried out the sors' bidding. The korensis were made eunuchs by the sors and were chosen at random in their infancy. Room and board was provided to them for life.

Beyond this circle of guardians spread the dwellings and farms and workplaces of the kors across the sloping plain of Tai-Raynee. Their homes were built of mud, straw and branches roofed in foliage or skins. In the southeastern third of the compass, the Fishers made their home in the forest along the banks of the River Eri. In the southwestern third the land sloped into wide valleys of partially wooded savanna that ultimately reached a great lake, the horizon of the Hunters. In the northern third, the land sloped upward in an open plain rimmed by the deep forest on the east and west. This, with its wide border of clay tiles, was the horizon of the Farmers.

No kor went to the staggering cliff where the land ended and the sky began, except for the sors. Each sor went once, alone, as his last initiation into the high order. He would find that northern edge, sit perfectly still on the brink of the Three Stin Cliff in the leaning grass, and look at the infinite churn of facets on the curving turquoise bottom of the world. He would eat five black giss, and before the day was over he would cut off his right thumb and cast it into the ocean, rendering worldly endeavor impossible to him so that his eyes were forever fixed beyond the Immurtai world, into the Unknowable and Infinite Truth.

The Hunters' homes were spread over grassy hills. Even though they were not allowed to grow food, little wild-looking gardens of giss were scattered between homes, and all silently respected whose gardens they were.

When Win arrived at his home, Sara, his wife, and Sannava, his fair daughter, were returning with baskets of fish and giss and berries and nuts from the other areas of Tai-Raynee. They were smiling: the baskets were heavy. The family brought the bounty into their home and Win kissed his wife. "I'm going over to Zen's. Tuton is going with me. Have much food for us all when we are done!" Win nodded tall, gripping his stomach, which growled. "Oh—if Azurel comes home from the crafting place, tell her we are over at Mimu's. She may want to come over."

Azurel

"I'm going, too," shouted little Erg, swinging furious figure eights on the beams of the roof.

"Get down from there, Erg," Sara said.

Erg launched through the air and landed in his father's arms, a giggling ball of fur. Win's laugh boomed through his chest. "I'll see you later, Precious," he said to Sara, and, with a kiss, he turned and left as Erg climbed around his neck and folded his arms on top of his head.

When the three reached the broad hill on which the strong home of Zen was built, Zen and his four sons were already working on the feast hall with many others.

Gray Char, the wiry old kor who had long ago taught Win and Zen the Way to Hunt and a few Other Ways, sat on a boulder in the shade of a broad-leafed tree beside the new foundations. Char was now a bard of hunting tales and a master of Hunter lore who spent his silver years teaching and remembering. His grandson, Anto, worked with the others as they raised the hall.

Jak, the member of their troop who had broken his leg during the hunt, sat in a splint beside gray Char, trading tales with him. There were no doctors among the *Koroshi,* and so Jak had drunk much wine before Char set his bone. His wife had bound it with splints according to Char's instructions.

"Hey!" Win yelled as he came up the hill.

"Grab an axe!" Zen answered as he hove his own into a log.

Zen's wife, Neon, a rounded, good-looking kiori with charming white stripes curling from the inner corners of her violet eyes across her cheeks and over her temples, gave Win and Tuton clay cups of juice, tweaking little Erg's ear. Neon was one of the most accomplished Hearthkeepers among all of the Hunters. "We need a lot more wood, Win!" she said, glancing at her proud husband apologetically.

"Why don't you chop down this tree instead of going all the way to the river for wood?" asked Win, pointing to the great tree under which sat old Char and broken Jak and in which now thrashed little Erg as he swung round the forking boughs.

"No," said Neon. "It will break the rain and wind from the feast hall."

"It's a good tree," agreed Zen.

"Good Other Way." Win gulped down the wine, handing the cup back to Neon. "At it, then!" he grunted, reaching for an axe.

"Careful now, kioros," Neon said.

"Ho, Win! Look what I brought you!" sang a far-off voice.

Rueez came trudging up the path to the house, panting like a wolf, dragging a bundle of branches three times his size on a travois made of heavy lumber. He dumped it all with a rolling crash and gasped, not quite standing up straight as he planted his hands on his knees. He winced and breathed for a while as Win and Zen roared laughter.

"Maybe just better than you deadweights could manage, eh?" Rueez wheezed, shaking a feeble fist at them.

"Rueez!" Win laughed. "Short on brains to make up for being short on muscles.

Eh, Zen?"

Zen shook his head. "Good job, Ru. Looks like good lumber. Give him some wine. Let's get back to work!"

Afterward, Zen, Neon, his four sons, Char, Char's grandson Anto, Rueez, and Jak, who was dragged on a travois, went over to Win's home for the Feast of the Fifth Day.

They ate, laughed, boasted and made lofty speculations on what the feast hall should look like when it was done.

The torches were lit and the juices were flowing as Anto and Sannava stepped outside. Anto looked hotly into Sannava's eyes, which were greener than the envious sky. Young Anto and the sleek, golden Sannava kissed each other and embraced, stroking each other's patterns of fur as though the designs were their own private secrets, their tongues dancing like flames.

Anto looked down at Sannava's pink nipples on the blond swells of her breasts and he touched the tip of one. Sannava ran her fingers hypnotically down the fur on Anto's spine. He laughed softly, kissed her mischievous eye that looked down at him as he hugged her and pressed a hand behind her as they pressed together. She felt him, burning, sending a chill through her. The green twilight blazed around them as Anto growled playfully, squeezing her hips and wrestling with her eyes.

Little Erg burst out the front door and bolted between their legs, shrieking laughter as he ran down the hill.

"Where are you going, brat?" shouted Sannava.

"To climb the Cinter!" little Erg cried. "Old Char said I couldn't!"

"Wait!" Sannava cried.

"He shouldn't. That's for sure," Anto said.

The sors sent the Korensis out of the cave. They seated themselves at the back of the cave on the high mantle of stone surrounded by the hemisphere of painted figures.

Tor, the tall, muscle-bound attendant who had been favored with the task on this Fifth Day, lit the dry manthril flowers and served the sors the black giss. Then he left to guard the cave's entrance.

The white sor, On, was the oldest. His fur had been turned completely white by the black giss. His eyes were like white opals though his eyelids and mouth were midnight black. Yet it was his fingerless right hand that was the symbol of his leadership, a grim scepter of his status and power. When it had come time to sever his thumb, On had cut all the fingers from his right hand, instead. He chewed the giss now with something that bordered passion, as his fellows followed.

The light grew thin as the air grew cold. The ancient symbols of the Immurtai world faded, their colors dulling on the cave's walls and melting in shadow. The sors watched the running kors, the springing antelopes, the winging birds, the reaching plants, the wriggling worm, the scrabbling beetle, the flying hordes, the snake and apes and even the legendary whale, which only two sors had seen, all swallowed in absolute darkness. With the shadow came Truth, Complete, Total, Unchanging, Inevitable, and Always, Before and After.

They journeyed long into the dark.

Sannava walked up the gently sloping paths toward the Cinter. Tallow torches multiplied in the deepening dusk as she loped through the homes of the Hunters. That it was somewhat rude of the Hunter folk to celebrate on the sors' day of fasting and night of reclusion was never mentioned. It had slipped quietly into the sanctity of tradition. Yet the kors knew some rather bold kor long ago must have started it. It was firmly entrenched now, however, and practiced by most kors in every province to some degree—and the sors could not stop it. Indeed, they seemed content to entertain it.

To the sors it made the least difference, in fact. As they chased the Truth through the black giss every Fifth Night, it was somehow fitting that they were mocked by common kors, who chased the lies of the Immurtai. They atoned for the *Koreshi* as their fellow kors transgressed.

Though the sors had never noticed, and would not care, on the surface this party tradition gave a rhythm to the days, a regular surge like the beating of a heart. Kors inclined to participate had a goal before them, to be reached in five days. There was always an excess built up, of fish, giss, meat and wine, which the Hunters made and distributed more bounteously than any other province. Since the amounts of stock were the same on the morning of the First Day, this surge had remained invisible to the sors.

"So what if it's obscene?" whispered Sannava to herself, feeling guilty suddenly under the shadow of the Cinter as she wandered through the darker, quiet homes of the Korensis. Some of Father's friends had said, like Zen, laughing Zen: "That's what holy kors are there for—so we can give them something to worry about!" He was a brave, happy kor, Sannava thought now, warmly. Zen was a great hunter; he killed with confidence and so he was more merciful. He, and of course her father, Jak and Rueez, were all fine hunters. And Anto...

Sannava dained about Anto with delight, happily putting her *Demurtai* into her Immurtai, if that's what her sister's word really meant. She had left Anto very disappointed at her father's house, where they would hopefully keep feasting and drinking and boasting until she got back. Perhaps daining was blasphemous, as Azurel boasted... But it was too much fun to be a sin, she dained.

She had had a little wine. It was the only way to keep up on nights like this. But now, as she approached the giant tower of stone, she worried about little Erg. Surely, she hoped, he didn't try to climb the Cinter as he had boasted bigly after stealing sips from Father's cup. Little Erg climbed trees splendidly, more splendidly than any of the other little children, but no kor could climb the Cinter. She feared for his safety with juices in his little kor head.

The sky deepened another shade as she walked over the little footpaths winding through the workplaces of the artisans.

Yellow stars pricked the sky over the Cinter. She stopped, folding her arms and looking at the jagged monolith above, shivering as the wine wore thin. Then, on the pale, shining grass before the cave, she saw a tiny shadow, running.

"Erg!" she shouted, but the shadow darted up, into the cave.

She scratched her head. Maybe the wine was not wearing thin, after all.

Finally, a huge Korensi left the cave and came down toward her, and she turned, frightened, and headed for home, hoping that the wine had tricked her eyes.

In a modest home by the River Eri in the fishers' province of Tai-Raynee, the father of a fishing family distributed the meat. It was a roast from one of the antelopes bagged by Zen's and Win's troop, brought to them by Azurel.

The fisher Urti was a solemn kor with narrow shoulders and a cautious hardness pressing his tough lips flat. There were fishers of greater renown, fishers who had caught prizes of legendary size and with celebrated skill. But Urti held himself above all of these. He could have been as great as any other fisher, or better, he was certain. But he decided it was unnecessary to prove things by actions. His gray eyes were unmoving and wide, knitted together by a decision that he had made long ago. He passed out the bowls to his family without words.

Silently, They Ate

Though the bowls were heavy this night, the fisher Urti had seen hardship and bounty coming and going with equal indifference over the years. And he had come to believe, and the belief was a burden, that in the long run it was only the *Koroshi,* and not any single kor, that had any lasting or real meaning. Since then, his eyes had been fixed on this constant through all the seasons they had witnessed and all the things that they had seen.

Urti had two sons. His eldest, Tor, was a favored attendant of the sors, but he was not present as he tended them inside their cave. His youngest son, Turi, was a crafter. Bowing his head now, his eyes downcast, Turi accepted a bowl of food from his father.

"Eat," Urti said, handing a bowl to Azurel. "Then it will be gone."

Azurel almost burst into laughter as he said it. But the impulse died in the cold glare of Turi's father. "Thank you," she whispered, averting her eyes, as Turi had done.

Silently, they ate. *As though it is another chore in the preservation of the Koroshi*, dained Azurel, and she reflected that the privacy of "daining" was what called for a name, even though it named something that was invisible. It was a secret room with a door that could only be opened with one's inner lips—a room where one was free to weigh things outside.

The meat was burnt, bland and terrible, but Azurel swallowed it, as though it were her duty. She looked through the silence at the gray, weary-looking kiori who was Turi's mother. She seemed harried by mounting, impossible toils. And yet, while acutely aware of her trials, she was not the least angered, either. In fact, she seemed agreeable, in a painful way.

Why was it that kors who did more seemed tireless and kors who did less seemed tired all the time, Azurel dained. Was it something they dained? There were mothers of ten children, big, loud, hungry children in the Hunters' province, who made candles and fermented wine and always seemed on fire with life. There were troop leaders who had unending tasks and decisions to make and all the problems of many kors to deal with, and yet still seemed full of energy. There were crafters who made twice as much as other crafters and still had time for other things. Yet none of them treated life like an injury.

Both Turi and Azurel had graduated to High Crafters, versed in all crafts. They had made pieces to be reviewed by the sors the day after tomorrow so that the sors could decide whether or not they could graduate to the highest level and be Artists. Traditionally, High Crafters were allowed to show their statue three times before their review on the three nights preceding it. Turi's statue was in the middle of the table before them.

Azurel finally laughed, unable to suppress a geyser of mirth. The other kors looked up at her, their faces plain as river stones. "I was just dain—looking at your statue, Turi. How dumpy and squat your kor is, with those beady eyes and that huge nose. And I must ask you—why is he so stubby and impossible? You are a better crafter than this, with better hands and better eyes, I know! I've seen your tools. You wanted to make his limbs so uneven and thick. Why, Turi?"

Turi looked at his plate, silent, with no intention of answering. He seemed more ashamed of the praise than the criticism as he turned his head from his father.

Urti stopped eating and looked at Azurel with his wide gray eyes that reminded Azurel of winter. "What has the *Demurtai* to do with the false shapes of the Immurtai?" Urti asked without asking.

Azurel looked at him, hesitating. "Well, yes, of course," she said, retreating to the other room. *How terrible*! she dained.

When the meal ended, she asked Turi to go back with her to her family's house, and, after Urti nodded, Turi went with her.

Azurel pushed the door in upon a loud chorus of the Star Song salted with Hunter alterations. The smell of spiced roast meat inside the home made Turi's mouth water.

Win stopped the song and the harmony burst apart like a shower of sparks. "Azurel, my daughter, and Turi, by starlight! Come, drink wine with us!"

Win rose and held out his arms, and they went to him and he crushed them both against his giant chest. Their hands were wrapped around cups and they were sat down and given dishes of succulent food.

"So, Azurel, your father tells me that, after being the best axe-maker and all-around tool-smith in Tai-Raynee, you will now be a very grand Artist," Zen said. "Show me your statues! I know the grip of your tools well enough."

Azurel left Turi at the table to fetch her statues. Turi looked at the kors crowded in the dining room as they whispered in anticipation, waiting for Azurel. "So, I hear you're an Artist, too," said Rueez, nudging Turi's shoulder.

Turi did not reply, for he was not yet an Artist, and neither was Azurel.

"You won't have to watch the holy shit anymore, eh?" laughed old Char, elbowing him. Artists lived at their own homes and did not have to work at the crafting places.

"What?" Turi was shocked at the question, his beard hot and his heart churning. He felt dizzy, and sick in his stomach.

Zen interceded. "Not at all, nothing at all, he meant not a thing by it, the old kor." He squeezed young Turi's shoulder.

Turi was shocked by the touch, but felt charmed for a moment after, before he resented it.

Azurel returned and she placed her two polished jade statues on the table.

One was a kioro with his arms bent outward, hands outspread on his chest. There was a sharp, unusual nose on his proud face, like that of Rueez. The other statue was a stunning kiori poised on one hip, her back arched. Not only did they look like splendid kors, they somehow looked better than kors.

Rueez looked at Azurel, and his frozen love for her melted in his eyes. She looked sadly at his proud eyes for a moment, then looked away.

Turi glowered at the statue of the kiori. It was exactly what one wanted a kiori to look like. No, it was what one *dreamed* a kiori could look like when one was asleep and could see what one wanted to see. He saw that both statues had been carved around red veins inside the glowing green stone. The candlelight gleamed in the curving grooves of fur patterned on the muscular figures, illuminating the pulsing stone. He saw Azurel's unashamed skill pushed to its very limits to show itself off. Turi looked at them, leaned intensely on them, as if they solved everything that was puzzling him. He looked away. "I've got to go," he said, rising.

"Sure, Turi. Sorry you can't stay," Azurel said, sadly.

"Why, these are beautiful statues, good strong statues, Azzy," Zen thundered. "I've never seen better!"

Turi left amid the boisterous praise of Azurel's statues.

Soon after, Rueez went outside.

Azurel went out to meet him.

He gripped her hands in his and wept.

Rueez, who was never afraid and laughed at pain, wept, and it wounded her, almost physically, to see it.

"Tell me why, again," he said.

Turi was listening from behind a tree.

"Rueez. Artists cannot take mates. They cannot touch the world that can be felt. They must devote themselves to higher things, to the *Demurtai*. It is the Way, my love."

"*Bah!* It's wrong!"

"If I gave it up, I would have nothing to give you but my Immurtai, dead as the meat we eat."

Rueez hung his head. "What kind of law is this? It cuts us in two."

Turi felt disgust and gladness to hear this hunter's words.

"Forgive me, Rueez! But you must forget me." Azurel turned, torn, and went inside.

Rueez shook his head. "No, never," he growled, and he set off for his lonely hut.

A mean brew of pain and pleasure drugged Turi's heart and he turned away and marched into the night toward his family's home.

Sannava came through the door right after Azurel. "Little Erg is missing, Mother!" she whispered in Sara's ear.

"Eh? Oh, I'm sure he'll be back by morning," said Sara, stroking silly circles in the back of Azurel's head as she praised her daughter's beautiful statues. "Some hunter family must have given him a bed when they saw how many sips he stole tonight. We'll tell him what-for come morning!"

"Yes, Mother," Sannava said.

II

It was the First Day, at dawn.

The family stood outside in the early morning fog before parting.

"Tuton and I are going on the hunt," Win said, shouldering his hunting kit. "Azurel, what are you doing today?"

"I was going to help Zen on the feast hall. I worked ahead on my crafts yesterday."

"Good girl!" Win smiled. "I was disappointed when you weren't there yesterday, and so was Zen."

"Win, little Erg is still missing," Sara said.

"Oh? Look around, then, you and Sannava. Maybe he's with some others this morning, with a headache. He was stealing sips last night. Goodbye, my family! Good travels today!" Win hugged Sara and Sannava and Azurel farewell.

Turi walked up the hill to Zen's house, eating a brown apple. He approached Azurel, who was pounding posts into the ground for the addition to Zen's house. "Why are you not at the crafting place, Azurel?" Turi asked. "I am eating now, so I came to see what you're doing."

"I worked ahead yesterday so I can work on Zen's feast hall," she said, smiling and catching her breath.

"Feast hall? I'm surprised Zen is building a feast hall. But why aren't you working on your statues? Tomorrow is your appeal to the sors."

"I have worked on them for two years. They are done," Azurel said.

"But—" Turi blurted, and he looked around at the others who worked on the hall. "This is very strange. How is it so many are taking away from work to build Zen a feast hall? Do the sors know?"

"They are Zen's friends. Zen and his hunters have worked ahead. My father and brother are hunting today to get further ahead so we all have more time for the feast hall. It's very good, don't you dain, Turi?"

"Me? What?" Turi frowned. He had heard that word but didn't know what it meant. "It's very strange," he said.

Azurel laughed. "Working ahead" was Zen's dain, and they all quickly accepted it for the sake of the hall. "I made 40 spears yesterday and a stone axe. Twice what you did, eh?" she said.

"Well, sure, that is."

"So. Now I can work here if I want. That's why I worked hard yesterday."

"Yes, well." Turi turned. "I'm going back to the crafting place to work on my statue."

"Goodbye, Turi. Good work!"

Turi frowned, disliking that Hunter phrase, and he turned, biting into the apple core as he left.

On the night of the First Day, Ez raised a question in the cave.

Often points of interest were reviewed by the sors.

"O! In the light of the golden Nuthany, and the Twelve Tiers, what are the signs of one those whose souls are merged with the *Koroshi,* and transcendence?"

This question was a common sort of question, intricate and demanding. A complete exposition was necessary. Ez sat back, relieved, awaiting the answer.

"Ez, one knows when one releases all of one's desire for Immurtai gratifications, which are fleeting. It is when one's mind is so purified that it is alone and finally able to merge with the *Demurtai,*" said white On, his fingerless hand resting on his knee.

"One who is unaffected by the miseries of the Immurtai and who is not filled with joy at the bounty of the Immurtai is truly *Demurtai* and a sage of sor's stature," said Iz.

"When passing through the Immurtai, it is the one who is unaffected by the plenty and the plague, neither pleased nor pained, who concerns himself only with the *Demurtai* and has truly reached the Perfect and the Forever Truth; he alone is at peace," said En, the only dark-haired sor, who was very old nevertheless. He was built unusually large and strong for a sor though his back was bowed from heavy decades.

"The soul that is trapped inside the Immurtai may be forbidden the excitement of the senses entirely, but there is a faint desire for the Immurtai that lingers," said Ez, requesting the extension of the answer.

"It is by transcending to a higher goal with no aim at oneself that one's soul is truly freed," said Pla.

"But the senses give such strong signals from the Immurtai world. It is enough to sway the mind of kors," said Ez, triggering the final stanza of the litany.

"While sensing Immurtai things, a kor will cultivate a certain attraction toward the Immurtai, and from such attraction lust develops, followed by anger," said white On, waving his maimed hand in a plaintive gesture, closing his eyes and grimacing at Ez's banality, as though it were smoke obscuring the clarity of the answer, or waves rippling the perfect mirror of silence. "After anger," he went on, "great irrationality follows, and the wits are scattered as one chases the chaos of the Immurtai world like leaves in the wind."

Ez bowed his head at the end of the customary reply. The cave was silent then, for many hours.

Holy Sor stared from the niche above them in the red light of the ring of coals. And when he slept Ez had a nightmare that night. He dreamed of the previous night that had already been swallowed by the past. He dreamed of the child and the blood and woke up shivering and soaked with the pungent sweat of his fear.

On the Second Day, the 22 sors sat cross-legged, gathered together on the grass mound south of the cave to judge two Pleas of Art.

No family of the two high crafters who were appealing them were permitted to watch. But many of the old, and the children, and those between toils, and other crafters, gathered before the Cinter to see the judging. Rueez had hidden himself among these now.

The grass waved in the thick, moist wind. The sun was bright gold as it tilted toward its bed.

"Daughter of Win, you are a crafter who makes knives and other subtle tools for the *Koroshi*. What is it, now, that you offer?" said Ez in the traditional address.

"I offer my art," she said.

This was not the traditional response, whose correctness was derived more from attitude and enlightenment than litany, but which the elect understood like a native tongue. Azurel's response caused immediate doubt.

"What is it that you find fit and holy to say of your frail senses, which is the thing that you find fit as an apology to the absolute Truth?" asked white On, the oldest sor, correcting Azurel's tone. He scratched his crotch with his fingerless hand, gazing at the sky.

Azurel stood confidently before him as she held up the jade figures. They glinted in the wind, bodies made of sky that seemed to catch the sun inside them. She waited for the sors to call for them so they could see and feel how subtle was her craft and see them with their own eyes.

One sor bent toward the audience and defecated in the grass.

Ez saw Azurel's statues and his eyes were dazzled. He wanted to see them closer, so he closed his eyes and spoke: "What does the son of Urti find fit?"

Turi, surprised, walked quickly to Azurel's side.

"I offer this. It is the honesty of my craft, after all. It is the hard bluntness of my skill which seemed mighty in a dream one night and then revealed itself humble to me so that this is the thing I offer as art."

Turi's statue was carved in coarse gray rock. Its arms, legs, buttocks and stomach, as Azurel moaned when she first saw it, were swollen and thick, its bones short and bent, its head overlarge and nose overfat and overlong. Its eyes were closed, its mouth open in a moan, its hands raised in front of its face, and its knees buckled on the palms of Turi's hands.

"Who was the model of this?" asked white On.

"Myself," Turi said.

Azurel looked at him.

"Azurel shall be forbidden from stabbing the heavens with her flesh-love and Turi shall be permitted to shape the eternal Truth for the *Koroshi*," white On said.

Ez nodded, eyes closed.

The kors moved away then, going about the chores awaiting them, and the sors strung out before the 22 stone blocks surrounding the Cinter to watch the sun, and another day, pass away.

"You don't see it, Azzy!" said Turi who stood by her as the sors and the gallery dispersed. "You just don't see the Truth. You get caught up in your own skin and cannot go farther and cannot see more! Most kors can't, so don't be discouraged. You love the wrong things to be an Artist. I could tell by your family that you never learned the things an Artist must know. It's not your fault!"

Azurel gazed at the barbed head of the Cinter, holding her statues in her golden hands.

"It takes something more—a surrender to Eternity, but anyway you just don't see it, and that's all. Nobody really can. But your whole family seems stuck on the moment and themselves… I would say they are almost Immurtai, Azurel. I'm sorry to say it…"

"Please don't talk about my family," she said, daining how she could tell them. She felt sick and weak. She felt numb, walking through the crowd of kors, who looked sadly at her.

"Well, don't worry about them!" Turi smiled. "I'll tell them about it for you, if you want. I'll tell them art is just not for you. I'll try to explain why to them, if I can. And anyway, I'll tell them you are a very good toolmaker and—"

"No!" said Azurel.

Turi smiled, looking kindly at her as they walked, wanting to rub her head to console her somehow, to help her just accept it. The universe seemed right again to Turi, and he no longer wished her any malice. He looked down and found himself sneering at the statues in her hands. No, it was not necessary to sneer. *You have won! They will be destroyed, forgotten, as though they never existed, like all art, like everything.*

A silver kor in the crowd stepped forward suddenly and clutched Azurel's wrist and smiled at her. "No," he whispered, shaking his head. She lifted the statue of the kiori and he looked at it in joy.

Turi shoved him away. "Simple old kor, run along!"

She approached the old kor. There were tears on his old face. "Never mind, old one. You saw them. Be happy," she said, and showed him the statues one more time before she turned away.

Turi hurried her along, continuing by her side all the way to her home, and he entered with her as she went before Win and Sara and Sannava and Tuton, who were eating dinner.

She stopped before the table, Turi standing beside her. The others looked at her as she set her statues on the table.

"Erg is still gone?" she asked them.

Win nodded.

For a long moment Azurel looked down at her statues, and tears full of their gleam rolled from her eyes. "Well, it was no," she said.

Turi watched. There were no words. The family bowed their heads in a silent storm of sadness.

For many moments Turi looked at them, waiting for them to speak or curse or carry on. But they did not. The family did not move, they hardly breathed. They just stared at the statues, so alive and happy and beautiful between them.

Turi looked away, a wave of sickness salting his mouth. He turned and quickly left the house.

As he hastened down the path, he heard Azurel call him, and he turned, scowling.

"Turi, I have something for you."

"What?" he snapped.

On Azurel's hands was a sheet of leather upon which lay a variety of tools. "I made these subtle tools for the carving of art. Now they are for you."

"Thank you, Azurel," smiled Turi in generous pity, taking the tools he knew he would certainly never need for his art.

"I am a crafter," said Azurel. "You are an Artist. There is no need to thank me." She turned and left him.

As Turi walked home his cruel love for Azurel bruised and blackened his heart. Somehow he felt smaller now. Somehow she had won.

"Tor, you are home," said Turi to his brother.

"Yes. The sors let me come home," Tor said.

"Tor, I have witnessed great Immurtai among the Hunters," Turi said.

"Oh?" asked Tor, who was tall, broad, and massed with muscle from lifting a stone over and over again.

"The father of Azurel and others near her are greedily working against the *Koroshi,* Brother, immersed in themselves and things. Dangerously so!"

"Slow down, Brother. You have mentioned that you did not like them. What have you discovered now?"

"One of them, whose name is Zen, is building a feast hall onto his house."

"A 'feast hall?' Those are queer words, a thing very much Immurtai, I think. And to use 'hall,' a word that only means the place where sors meet. That is forbidden, I am certain."

"Yes!"

"A hunter, you say, who is named Zen?" Tor asked.

"Zen and others neglect their work to build this 'hall.' They are crazy with the passing things, Brother, they cling to sticks and hoard the crackar Immurtai things! They care nothing for the far wisdom of the sors!" Turi's sharp gray tongue flicking over his yellow teeth.

"I thank you, brother, for this." Tor nodded. "The sors are pleased with your art. It is truly a beautiful and transcendent offering that you made to the *Demurtai*. The sors were admiring it this very evening. I believe it soothed them, greatly."

Turi smiled, turning his head. "Thank you, Tor."

The brothers looked uncertainly into each other's eyes for a moment, and as they turned away they knew their future.

"Masters, there is sin festering."

"Which and whose?"

The tall and mighty Tor stood in an easily buffeted stance, his hips apprehensively tilting subtly to the left or right, his shoulders as easily repositioned, his arms and hands hanging in readily readjusted angles, as though he did not know how his muscular limbs should hang but was willing to rearrange them and unwilling to let them hang contrary to any whim of the sors, whom he respected and secretly loved.

The sors had always been quietly approving of Tor. Tor's father was a loyal kor who reported on many a neighbor who indulged the Immurtai.

"Zen, a friend of Azurel who proposed obscenity as art, is a hunter who already has four sons. He is building a hall for dining, into which he will bring his friends to drink, cavort, and indulge on the far edge of Tai-Raynee."

"A *hall*?" The unknown use of this word was more distressing than the object it might describe. The sors exchanged quick glances.

"Larger than any other building," said Tor. "And they are calling it a 'hall.'"

"We shall walk out tomorrow and see the doings of this kor, who builds overmuch and fornicates overmuch and whose friends love obscenity and Immurtai things," On nodded.

"I shall inform the Korensis." Tor bowed, and he left the cave.

The next day after the hunt, Zen and his sons, along with Win and Sara and Tuton and Azurel, and old Char and broken Jak and some of his youngsters, and Anto and Sannava, went over to Zen's house to fit the skins over the roof of the feast hall. Zen finally had enough skins to line the roof double-thick, as he had wanted.

Neon brought out bowls of bean nuts, dried figs, raw fish, and wine.

"Mimu, catch!" said little Jeek, Jak's son.

Zen noticed just in time to catch a bean nut on his nose. "Win! We need a monkey to climb the roof and pull some cords over. Is little Erg about yet or do I have to trust this little muskrat?"

"No, Zen, he's not about yet."

"Oh." Zen frowned. "I'm sorry to hear that. All right, then, Jeeky. Will you pull this end over the roof to the other side?"

Jeeky jumped up and down and grabbed the cord as it was handed to him, putting its end in his teeth. He jumped onto the edge of the A-framed roof and scampered over the vaulted framework, landing on the ground on the other side.

Win and Sara looked sadly at Jeeky, and Win squeezed Sara's hand.

Zen's sons took the cord from Jeek, after a short but frenzied chase, and Zen told them to pull. They hoisted the first patchwork section of hides over the roof. There was much applause when it was done, and everyone paused to drink wine and make comments.

"It's a brave and good building," Char said, his gray eyes young.

And the kors agreed.

"Don't feel bad," Zen said, noticing a dejected Azurel. "I'll build a place for your beautiful statues on the hearth. And you can make as many more as you like and I will proudly show them in the feast hall! You could marry Rueez, then, and still make art for Hunters. I hope you make as many statues as the stars!"

"Somehow," said black Kon, "we'll just say you're a hunter now and hide you away, so you can make art just for Hunters. Eh, Char?"

"Yes," Char nodded.

"We'll work something out," Zen winked. "It'll have to be kept secret. But we Hunters excel at that!"

Azurel hugged Zen, too overcome to speak.

Tuton and Win lashed the hide to the roof frame with leather straps and long bone needles made by Azurel, as Zen spoke to Jeek about pulling another cord over the roof.

Iz, Ez, and On approached the hill on which the hunter Zen lived.

The three sors walked slowly up the path. They did not speak or look at one another as they neared. Fifty Korensis marched behind them.

Zen noticed them and motioned the others to stop. "Jak, leave," Zen said. Jak nodded and hobbled indoors to hide.

Zen turned to face the sors and their guards on his hill.

"You are Zen, a Hunter who slays and guts beasts?" asked On. His fur was white as a cloud. Zen noticed his right hand. All the fingers had been cut off.

The sor looked at Zen through milky, motionless eyes. "You are the hero Hunter who believes he can cheat death, and hide behind the crackar—and your name is Zen?"

"I am Zen," Zen said.

"What are you building?" Ez said.

"It—" He smiled at the others. "It is a feast hall, master."

"A feast hall!"

Zen frowned. "Yes."

"Guards," said On gently. "Take down the Immurtai and disperse it throughout the *Koroshi* to end this blasphemy."

The hunters stared as the guards took down the skins they had just raised, cutting the cords with knives.

"You are concerned only with the Immurtai," whispered white On. "You were trying to build a feast hall. A place to gorge and languish in crude deceptions." The sor's eyes were fixed on a purple cloud spreading over the sky.

Zen looked around. "No! This hall is not so much sap, so much timber. It is *Demurtai*!" he blurted. "A dream, like so, eh?" He tapped his thick-furred head and snapped his black fingers. "*More* than the wood is mine. More, I tell you! And you take more with you than wood," he growled, gesturing anxiously at the spiral galaxy on his chest.

White On opened his mouth, but only stared at Zen for a moment. "It is these crackar things that are not important, Hunter," he finally said. "Do not presume to teach us. It is you who must learn."

"Why do you concern yourselves, then?" charged Zen. He waved his huge arm at the kors who took axes to the hall behind him.

The white sor smiled, amused at Zen's desperation. He looked at the five black knobs on his right hand. "It's the *Demurtai,* and not the Immurtai, with which we are concerned, kor."

"Master?" said the gray hunter, Char, his weathered brows furrowed. He turned over his own strong-sinewed fist. "May I give you a question?"

On sighed. "In answer to your first question, you may, old kor."

"Why do we live?"

"There is no why, old kor, if it is not Eternal. We are nothing if we lose ourselves in the passing things, the crackar things."

"These things—" began Azurel.

"Things, Kiori!" Ez hissed bitterly, recognizing the crafter.

"These things are life! Surely, use your eyes and see them," said Char.

"One thing leads to more things, and more, old kor, more things than you can ever see with your feeble eyes. Soon there are never enough things and kors will forget the infinite Truth so that they may have things! And the millions of things will split kors in different directions and tear them from the higher Truth and all will cry for freedom from that which is so much greater than themselves. Do you believe we have not seen where the Immurtai world might take us? Forget the stone and the grass and the wood that surrounds you! If you chase it, it dies, and you must run harder to catch more. Then you die, like all other things, and you will never have known the Truth."

"Masters, what truth do you speak of?" Char asked.

"The Forever Truth, kor!" Ez said.

"I tell you there is no such thing. Nothing is eternal, not even the stars. Forever is now and always will be. Life is something, not everything. It is only so big, so heavy, so long, so placed, like the wind, like the grass, and the stones: Why do you hate this? Why don't you love it, as we Hunters do?"

"Old kor, your tongue might do better if removed from your head. Such words are infernally ignorant," said white On. "Do not speak therefore in the future, except to grandson for drinking water, or grandmother for toilet roughage or the tongue will be cast away, into Forever, where it will finally speak the Truth. Now to this..." On waved his truncated hand. "Will strangers share this 'hall' of Zen?"

"Some, always," said Zen, who met kors proudly and happily.

"Will friends be treated more than strangers?"

"Yes," Zen growled impatiently.

"You are indeed Immurtai," nodded white On. His eyes seemed to be focused on a very great distance over Zen's head and past the clouds and even past the first stars that were appearing. "It is you who are concerned with the Immurtai, Hunter. It is not the courtship of certain kors that pleases the Amoli, the Entirety. How foolish can you be? Features and characters built on decaying fabrics are as false as the weathers and the antelopes that you slay daily. You should know this, more than others. The *Koroshi* is Truth, hand in hand with God and Eternity. Do you intend to bring calamity by this shortness of sight? Do you want to steal the Truth from the *Koroshi*? Do you want the Truth to live on when your crude flesh is broken or to die too wrapped in decaying tissues to escape? Do you want to keep your hall? Then ask only strangers in each night."

Zen looked at them, confused. "No." He shook his head.

"Tear it down—completely down—and disperse it across Tai-Raynee so that it might serve the *Koroshi* and not challenge it," On said.

"Tear it down!" said Ez.

And as the Korensis tore down the hall, the sors left, even as the fine ash of night fell over the Immurtai world.

Win's family returned home. They moved into the dark dining room.

Tuton lit two tallow candles and Sara put away a basket of bean nuts that Neon had given her. Sannava and Azurel closed the windows with elk hides and paused for a moment afterwards, facing each other, before retiring to their bedrooms.

Sara suddenly touched Win's arm. "Little Erg is still gone!"

Sannava touched his other arm. "Father?"

"Yes?"

"The night he disappeared, I thought I saw him running up into the cave!"

"What? How did Erg go that way?"

"He said he was going to climb the Cinter. He was foolish with wine!"

Win's eyes narrowed. "Very well. We shall have audience with the sors on this thing come the Fifth Day. For now, let us rest, my family."

Early in the morning on the Fourth Day, Zen climbed the tree that was to break the wind and rain from his hall. He lay across its boughs, a giss gourd of juice in one hand, ignoring Neon's calls, as he got drunk.

Dawn washed the western sky and Zen sat chuckling bitterly on the bending branches when a bird fluttered into the tree before him. It was a green parrot with twigs in its beak. It wove them into its basket-nest on a high branch. Zen laughed, a long, thunderous, staccato wail that staggered over sleeping Tai-Raynee.

Tears brimmed in his hard blue eyes. He grabbed a branch in his right hand and squeezed it and the branch's leaves trembled. For a moment he wanted to rip it from the tree and drive it into the soil, the corner post of a new hall: but he could not. He could not do this simple thing. The parrot owned this world, but he did not.

Too many ropes tied his soul to this green land and the things all around him. Now all these nerves had been cut and he drank the wine to blur his senses and numb the phantom pain of these endless missing limbs. He roared angrily at the parrot building its nest, and it fluttered into the sky and shrieked: "The Truth is in Tai-Raynee! *Raaak!*"

It startled him, and Zen fell from the tree, landing on his back in the grass.

Neon ran to him.

He lay his head on her knee. "A bird was mocking me!

Zen!" Neon kissed his brow and somehow got him to his feet.

The Truth Is in Tai-Raynee

She put Zen to bed and went outside, weeping to see her husband so lost.

And she looked at the sky for the evil bird that had spoken. But it was gone.

Azurel lay against Rueez in the long grass beside the River Eri.

Rueez held her breasts, as though protecting them, but she seemed wounded from within as she looked at the statues in her hands. Tomorrow they must be broken, as was Tradition. It was as though she must go, tomorrow morning, to have her head cut off, and she wept in cold fear for her life, for Rueez, for the world itself, which would never be loved by her hands. Perhaps it was evil to wrap oneself too much in the Immurtai world, she dained, as the sors said. Perhaps the cause of the *Koroshi,* because it was unreachable and unspoilable, was the best cause for kors. Perhaps daining was evil, she dained, bitterly.

She felt Rueez's strong chest trembling against her back.

He stroked her head soothingly, hiding his own pain.

"You can have me, Rueez," she said.

"*Shhh.* What is there to have?"

She looked up at him. "Tonight, I will live. Tonight your flesh will be my obscene clay, and your hands my sinful inspiration. I will make my last piece of art out of you before my heart dies."

His tears salted her lips as he kissed her, and they made a lifetime of love that hour, with love that was more revenge than celebration, more defiance than joy, hidden in the reeds beside the gossiping river.

It was dusk when Win and Sannava walked to the edge of the winding River Eri. Her father was silent on the walk, and when they reached the bank he flung little stones on the smooth green water as she waited. Sannava knew he wanted to tell her something but was letting some great pain pass first. She sat in the grass on the bank, looking at the Brown Ducks and Black Geese paddling between the reeds. Her father stood twelve hands tall, his broad back turned to her as he skipped flat pebbles.

Win looked at the southern horizon. He feared that Little Erg, his son, his bright jewel, brighter than the stars in heaven, had somehow been lost.

He stared at the few golden stars over the southern horizon as the crickets played their flutes, and he saw a strange glow emanating from the horizon. The tears must be playing tricks on his eyes. He hung his head and brushed them away into the stream.

He turned to his patient daughter. "My daughter, I am sorry."

It was too dark for her to see Win's eyes, but the sound of his voice made tears spill from hers. He shook his head, his strong arms limp and weak.

She hugged him, pressing her face to the diamond on his chest. "You didn't make the world, Daddy," she whispered.

Late in the afternoon on the Fifth Day, Win finished his work and struck off toward the Cinter with Sara, Sannava, Azurel, Tuton, and Zen, who also intended an audience with the sors about the hall, along with his four sons, Neon, and Rueez.

In an hour they walked the two stins to the Cinter and approached the 22 sors gathered on the mound before the cave. The sors sat in a semi-circle before two farmers in dispute. Many had gathered to hear them. Armed with ceremonial long-handled stone axes, 220 Korensis stood still and silent to each side of the sors.

Dusk fell as the audience before Win finished, and Win quickly walked up to the sors as the farmers left. He addressed them as his own family and Zen's listened.

"Masters," Win said, nodding his head in recognition. "I come to ask you of my son."

"Speak," On said.

"My little son, on the last Fifth Day, has been missing. My daughter tells me she saw him running into the cave as night fell. Do you know an outcome to this?"

The crowd stirred and whispered at Win's back.

The sors did not look at each another.

"Your son broke an eternal silence," Ez said.

The other sors did not show their surprise at Ez's statement.

"To atone this grave trespass he became part of that silence," said Ez.

Night descended as the lavender planets were rising.

"He was silenced for a reckless, arrogant, and ignorant act," said white On, waving his club hand, annoyed at Ez's pretension. He suspected the sor's remorse. "He did come into the cave, whereupon he broke the silence and denied the knowledge of Sor."

Win grimaced, staggering back. "Masters, what compelled him? Did he tell you?

He said that God was dying and falling from the sky," Ez said as he remembered that night against his will, though it should have been swallowed by the Past. But he remembered and could not forget. As though driven by a single nerve, the sors' left hands had worked the boy's body in a ritual of motions, pulling, pushing with mechanical precision, like a natural process, like the day-by-day relaxation of decay or the erosion of a river's banks as each joint had been snapped by practiced fingers with exacting pressure. As if the boy's body were nothing but a chain of childish puzzles undone by simple tricks, they undid him until all that was left were nails, fur, hands, feet, limbs, ribs, dull black eyes, a small, gleaming skull—the Twelve Tiers of personal identity, meaningful only in their meaninglessness before the forever Truth, before they were thrown into the Infinite Past. The massive, patient Past, recited Ez as he looked at his missing thumb and sweat poured cold down his back. The Past and Future, Ez repeated to himself, where the false present could no longer mock the *Demurtai*.

Win stood on the slope of the mound looking up at the sors as the northern wind whistled around the Cinter. Little Erg had been full of wine, he thought. Win punished himself for the tragedy. Little Erg had trespassed high things in his feckless journey, and the fault was Win's. He turned, glancing at Sara, and through his tears he saw a glow on the southern horizon. "Masters," he said, "I am most sorry to hear this! I must take my family away from here." Grief overcame him, and he turned away, walking down the hill toward Sara.

He took Sannava's and Azurel's hands in his and kissed his wife. Zen gripped his shoulder, glaring at the sors in stark rage.

The sors whispered among themselves as a gasp spread over the field.

Zen and Win looked south. The bleeding star finally rose over the southern horizon, huge and frozen in the sky even as it seemed to be leaping like a golden ghost.

Many kors kneeled down in the grass before the vision, and the children cried in fear as a liquid plume streamed long behind the glowing specter. It had a bright and laughing face with limbs cast back, so like the image of his son when he leaped through the air that Win found himself smiling in wonder. Then he remembered the glow he had seen the night before in the south. Erg had told the truth!

His little son had climbed the Cinter, after all, and had seen this fiery phantom before anyone else and tried to warn the sors!

Win wheeled on the sors now as they gasped in terror. "My little boy was heady with wine, it's true!" he cried. "And his heart was pretty as he read the world. And so were you conjuring dreams as you followed the black giss through the workings of heaven. But it was my boy, my little, stupid boy who saw this demon in heaven while you saw nothing! Better served is Tai-Raynee by a dreaming boy with open eyes, I say, than 22 old kors cowering in a cave!" Win shook his square fist as rage bettered him in that moment.

"My ghost will rise as big as Forever," remembered Ez as he cringed before the weeping spirit leaping over the southern horizon; for he saw the same likeness Win had seen, though to him the ghost of little Erg was not laughing but crying golden tears that bled a golden stream behind it.

Kors swooned across all of Tai-Raynee before the specter in the sky as Zen ran up the slope to reach Win's side—but at the motion of white On, the Korensis converged on Win in the thickening darkness.

Win's hand snatched the wrist of a Korensi as another swung down his long axe. He tore the guard's arm from its socket even as his own right hand fell to the ground, severed, still clutching the Korensi's wrist. A crowded thud of axes gashed Win's back and blackness much deeper than the night came over his sight as he fell, and as he lay in the grass his last vision was of his son smiling back at him in the distant sky.

The white sor rose to his feet, golden in the comet's glow, and he raised his fingerless hand to calm the crowd as Win's family and Zen's howled below. "This sign in heaven is a warning," white On cried, his high, chafing voice scraping the sky. "Great Immurtai grows within the *Koroshi*. This fantastic fire is the ghost of Sor avenging our sins. Only by restoring Faith in the *Koroshi* may the Heavens forgive our rebellion from the Truth. Go to your homes. Look for the wickedness in your hearts that has brought this evil over Tai-Raynee. Look hard, kors! The ghost of Sor will be merciless on those who follow the treachery of this kor. The Truth shall prevail, without those who defy it."

Then the sors told the Korensis to gather their numbers and deliver the sky's tidings to each house across Tai-Raynee.

Sara wept madly, shaking her head, her eyes blinded by grief.

Neon embraced her as Zen ran back to them.

"We shall go back," Zen said to Neon. Then he lifted Sara's chin and looked into her eyes. "And we shall go away!" he said.

Sannava wept beside Sara, and Tuton bellowed.

"Sara, I want you to meet me as soon as possible at the tannery," Zen said. "I am going now to raise the Hunters. We will leave this mad place, far behind us! Now is the time. This is the sign!"

"Yes, Zen," said Rueez, looking for Azurel.

Azurel stared at the cruel silhouette of the Cinter against the stars. And then, before Rueez saw her, she sprinted away through the churning crowd.

Zen ran furiously through the province of the Hunters and, with his sons, he spread the tidings of the sky to the hunter families before the Korensis could muster their numbers and spread the sors' pronouncement.

Fear had swept across Tai-Raynee. The hunters found kors wailing on their knees at the heavens, holding out their arms and grimacing before the smoldering, streaming star leaping over the southern horizon. Each of the hunting families was stunned by Zen's news and great anger filled the places in their hearts where they had love for Win.

"This is the ghost of little Erg, the Hunter child," Zen told them. "The son of Win!" They all looked sadly at the sky, having heard of Win's remarkable son, who Zen now told them had been murdered at the hands of the sors. And Zen won the will of many strong hunters, who gravely grasped his hands, sensing that the time to leave Tai-Raynee had finally come. They in turn sent out their children to tell the news and ask more Hunter families to meet at the tannery.

Sara, Sannava, and Tuton went to their house to pack their most essential belongings. Azurel was not at the house when they reached it, and her statues were gone.

In the darkness of the tanning place, as the blazing comet sank beneath the southern sky, over a thousand kioris and kioros now looked to Zen to confirm or disprove the tales they had heard.

"This light is little Erg?" asked gold Pog, a troop leader. "I heard he was a beautiful child."

"This light is our torch, Pog," Zen said. "It is our hope to find our own way, at last!"

The Hunters were a close-knit clan who shared a way divorced from all Tai-Raynee. Yet many declined to leave when Zen asked them now, including gold Pog. Instead, they bade him good luck and swore fidelity to him before the sors. And they wept to see so many beloved kors departing on that cruel night.

The 200 families that remained with Zen at the tannery were headed by proud kioris and kioros, who trusted the words of Zen, because they knew he loved the ways of the Hunters as they did.

"Mimu," asked Kon, one of the Wanto Warre. "What would you have us do to answer this villainy? Shall we attack the attacker, and kill the killers?"

Zen knew the future was pregnant with twins. The world could be turned upside-down by attack or by retreat. "No, Kon. It would be foolish to attack the sors, as it would be foolish to remain in Tai-Raynee," he said. "Both would mean death for Hunters. There has been too much death, already." Zen looked at the sky. "We shall leave!" He smiled, but there was a tragic gleam in his eye before the comet. "We will take as many hides as we can from the tannery!" he called to the families. "And the travois on which we may carry food and tools. All those mothers with infants I must ask to leave their babies with trusted friends. Our journey will be hard. The sors are sending Korensis throughout Tai-Raynee in search of this sort of thing, I guess! So we must be clever in our preparations and unseen. Use no paths the Korensis would know. Meet me at Sky-pit in two hours, hunters. And we will find a new home where we are free to live the life we love!"

And so, after nine millennia, urged by a giant ghost in the sky, kors prepared to leave the wheel of Tai-Raynee in search of a new horizon.

Resolved behind the challenge of Zen, the hunters separated, and, in despair, Rueez ran to every place he could dain to find Azurel.

Azurel ran up the terraced farmland above the Cinter in the night. A cold wind blew down the great slope before her now, carrying clay dust that stung her nose and eyes and clogged her windpipe. She clutched her jade statues in her hands as she bowed her head, and ran.

She only stopped at a group of storage houses to fill a strap-basket with white giss. Then she slung it over her shoulder and continued climbing the terraced fields, running over the flat spaces, climbing, and running again. She ran without regard for her limbs, driving them harder than she should have, though the pain was less than the pain inside her. She did not stop for seven stins.

Staggering past the last homestead, she fell in the fields beyond Tai-Raynee among the painted palettes of the sors, the crumbling "Days." She lay on the red shards, staring at the sky as she chewed white giss. Her mind was stunned, limping, meek.

When morning came she got up on her aching legs, and she ran again up the vast grid of discs toward the edge of the world, where, three stins down, a turquoise sea was said to lie, the Sea of the *Koroshi,* of which mere kors could only dream. *A perfect place to end,* she dained: the end of the world.

Rueez arrived last at Sky-pit, his brow low, his mouth loose, his eyes lost. Nevertheless, he stood firm by Zen's side.

"We shall go into the forest beyond the great lake," Zen called. "No kor has ever gone there. We shall be safe there, for a while." From Sky-pit, the ancient diamond quarry of the Hunters, Zen and the hunters of Tai-Raynee set grim eyes on the sloping lands below. They shouldered their heavy travois, the hearthkeepers tending the children and setting the pace, as they walked quickly south, the orange moon lighting their way.

"You've never been in that forest?" asked Zen of old Char.

"No," Char said. "But there is a legend. It is said that a crazy white kor lived in that forest, maybe three centuries ago. It's only a legend passed down through the Hunters."

"A white kor?" Zen grunted. "A strange tale…"

"Well, it was long ago," Char said.

"We should be safe there now," said Rueez. "Mimu?"

"Eh?"

"What will we do?"

Zen smiled. "What is right for us. From now on, Rueez. Don't be afraid."

The families of the hunters moved in stealth through the night and continued the next day. They finally slept without shelter the following night as a hard rain fell. At dawn, several of the children were fevered.

Zen and his four sons carried them on their shoulders as they moved on, in the direction of the leaping star that had risen in the southern sky. They stopped at noon and ate a quick meal of nuts and jerky as the sky clouded gray with a few patches of green. Sun and rain intermingled over them the rest of that day as they moved on, filled with misgivings and fear. They ate meagerly that night, and the new mothers shared their milk with the younger children. It was a cold night, but the rain had mercifully passed.

In the morning, Zen led the others east to the river. For a while, the kors stared at the fat fishes hovering in pools at the river's edge.

"If only we knew the ways of the Fishers," said Kon, rubbing the top of his ebony-furred head.

Some kors pathetically tried to use sticks like the spears of Fishers, and tried to stick snails on the point of sticks to lure the fish.

Then Zen grunted and walked into the rushing waters. He stamped about, perplexing the others, and with quick swats he slapped five fish onto the bank where the other kors grabbed them.

"I guess the fishers haven't tried any Other Ways for a while," he grunted, with a gruff laugh. "Come, hunters! You can herd them, just like elk!"

As the hunters followed Zen's example, the hearthkeepers prepared the raw fish. And soon the kors were sated and they moved on along the banks of the river now toward the lake, camping that night on its northern shore.

And the 200 families built bonfires from branches they gathered on the wooded banks of the river, and they gathered around the flames, pressed close, as they sang songs as cooked fish on sticks. Zen spoke to them.

"Do not fear, Hunters!" he said. "We shall find a place to our greatest liking, and there we will live to our greatest liking, and we will soon forget the sors and their ways. Their words are not here, somehow. And their hearts were never with us. They are in some other place. It is best, this way. And maybe, someday, we will return to Tai-Raynee so that we may bring change to that place."

The Hunter folk were happy at Zen's words. And they slept with bright and tumultuous dreams that night.

But Sara was awakened by Sannava sobbing. She touched her arm softly. "Daughter, it is hard," she said. "I tell myself Win is alive, but he is not! How can we go on with hearts in the past? We must live without him, for you know it is what he would have said to us, if he had words for us at the end."

"Erg and Azurel!" said Sannava.

Sara looked at her sternly, a hot tear burning her cheek. Her daughter Azurel… Yes, she would take her life. Azurel had loved life too deeply, even tiny wildflowers. All her world must have died to know that Erg and Win were dead. "We will never know," Sara said, and she stroked Sannava's head, looking at the ghost in the sky that looked so like her little Erg, leaping in the southern sky.

Azurel's eyes blurred as she stumbled up the great plain.

The slope grew steeper and the horizon above her, unlike other horizons, grew nearer as she pushed on. The field blended with the sky as her mind dulled with exhaustion. All she could feel were two strings of pain on her inner thighs and kneecaps.

She fell, finally, under the sun, laughing sadly and chewing giss as she rolled onto her back. The air was thin and the wind was strong on this moist high field.

She looked at the glowing blossoms of wildflowers bobbing over her, sprouting between the ancient Days which grew older as she ran farther, the senseless finger-strokes of past sors increasingly faded. She drifted into a deathly sleep.

She woke at a cold wind in the late afternoon, and she jumped up, running with a renewed vigor. She passed from the Days into blue-green rushes waving like a lake around her. She saw the edge, at last.

The brink of grass cut straight across the twilit heavens, which were purple now as the sun set. She fell to her knees with her statues in her hands, and she crawled up the slope to peer over the brink as stars slid up behind the blades of grass.

An arm's length away from the edge, Azurel was still unable to see the ocean that supposedly lay ten miles below. She rolled onto her back and looked at the shimmering sky.

She wept and laughed, unsure herself which she was doing. A glow appeared on the sky at the bottom of her eyes, and, looking down, she saw the comet leaping frozen over the tiny shadow of the Cinter. Azurel smiled, laying her head in the grass. She rolled onto her stomach, tears rushing hot from her eyes. *No more daining.*

She sprang over the edge of the cliff.

In the morning, Char showed Jak how to walk with a special cane he had made. By the end of breakfast, Jak was ready to walk with the other kors.

They reached the lake and saw great herds of antelope on the far shore before the unknown forest, and the hearts of the Hunters were warmed.

That day they almost circled the lake and camped on its southwestern shore about a stin-and-a-half from the wild wood.

In the night, a thick storm burst over the lake, driving rollers high on the beach. The kors huddled under the hides that they had brought.

In the morning, however, they found a clearing sky. Beneath it, on the sandy beach, crawled thousands of red crawfish, driven ashore by the high surf. They gathered up many and boiled them over small fires, relishing the savory meat.

By noon, they reached the south shore and, as they preparing to enter the tall forest, Rueez pointed out something on the edge of the trees some distance to the east.

It was a great square block of wet stone, weathered and rounded.

Zen brought the people to its side. There were deep gouges, like the scratch of a yellow sloth, in the rock. The boulder was three times as tall as Kon.

The kors entered the forest here, beside this strange rock, heading south.

Zen, Rueez, and Kon, the last three of the Wanto Warre, and Tuton, Win's son, went ahead of the main group in probing directions, calling out so the others could follow between.

"Another boulder," cried Tuton after the families made their way three stins into the thick and overgrown woods.

Zen, scouting with Rueez some distance away on a knoll, knitted his brow. "Stop!" he roared. He shrugged at Rueez's inquisitive expression. He rejoined the others and gathered the scouts, bringing them all to the place where Tuton had found a second boulder. It was roughly the same size as the first and square-shaped, though it was overgrown with roots and moss and orange orchids.

"No, Zen. It's impossible," said gray Char, scrutinizing the brooding Zen.

"Let us continue from here," said Zen. "Scouts, split up!"

They traveled another stin through the rain-damp forest as the sun dried the air when Zen came across another great, square-shouldered rock. He grinned for a moment before he called the others.

"Impossible!" said Char, peering into Zen's eyes.

"How far would you say these stones are from each other, Char?"

"I would say about one stin, or very close."

"Let us proceed from here," Zen called.

They traveled south for another seven miles, about two stins, when the excited voice of Char called the scouts together.

The main group had come across a giant square boulder, half-buried in the side of a tree-covered knoll.

Char laughed when he saw the eager light return to Zen's eyes. "You're crazy, Zen," he smirked.

The others could not follow their ongoing conversation.

"Nevertheless, let us continue from here, in the same direction," Zen said, shrugging at Char.

The scouts split up as the forest floor began to rise. Small root-choked hills made the ground irregular, so the scouts could not fan out so widely before the party. Zen sent the youngsters aloft to look for boulders from the branches above. Laughing and playing, the youngsters thrashed in the trees as the hunters moved forward.

They trekked through the forest for a long time without finding another boulder. The children had not spotted anything either, so Zen called them down. The shadow of dusk was thickening and they could see the comet rising through the branches. Then, finally, they reached a small clearing near the top of a ridge.

"What, ho!" Zen cried. He turned to Kon, Char and Rueez. "What say you now?" he boomed, slapping Char on the back.

The other kors hissed, and they bared their teeth.

"What say you, Zen?" whispered old Char, his silver brow furrowed.

Zen spread his hands.

A slender, squared stone fifteen arms tall stood in the center of the clearing. Four heavy megaliths stood around it, half as tall as the central dolmen. The evening hung heavy and purple in the glade as a brown rabbit foraged weeds by the central stone. The megaliths, although they were not 20 arms in front of them, seemed very far away, their distant purpose now blurred by the unforgiving hand of nature.

The depths opened beneath her, the turquoise sea swinging into view below, curved and engraved with a filigree of starshine. The cliff soared past her as she fell over the sea looking out at the brass-yellow stars in the twinkling sky that she would soon lose forever. She looked at the sculptures of kiori and kioro in her hands, glinting over the dark green sea. Soon they would be safe, with her, under the waves, forever.

She could see other tall, chalk-white cliffs across the emerald water, changing shape as she regarded them. The wind was violent against her and growing warmer as night fell. Azurel closed her eyes and sucked in a long breath as the wind pummeled her body. She went to the secret room inside her head, waiting for the end.

A strong arm of hot wind surged from a vast cavern that suddenly gaped open in the side of the cliff, lifting her up and slowing her fall just as she struck the shrugging crest of a high wave.

The wave pulled her down and up from its trough, cradling her on its white edge as it sped forward, laying her on a bed of cobblestones under a blanket of bubbles.

Stunned, she lay there for a moment as the wave subsided.

Then she climbed to her feet.

Was she dead? Was she a ghost? She set down her statues and felt herself in doubt.

The salty scent of the sea was strange and new to her. In the darkness, she made out a river of cobblestones issuing from the giant cave in the base of the Three Stin Cliff. The ceiling was at least a stin above her, a starless night that covered half the sky.

The cavern bored deep into the cliff and the rounded stones rose in a gray, snaking swath into the gloomy distance. A cobblestone cracked under her foot. She looked down at it. It was a skull.

Beside it gazed another, and another.

She lifted her eyes and fell to her knees.

The bones of a million kors poured out of the dark hole in the world into the infinite sea.

"It is the work of giants!" said Rueez as they looked at the stone monument, his eyes as round as two white giss.

Zen scoffed. "It is the work of proud things," he said. "That is all. We could shape rocks and raise them in this way. But for the sors it is Immurtai to stake such a heavy claim on the world." Zen's mouth wrenched as though tasting bad meat as he mentioned them.

"These queer menhirs are ancient, Zen," Char said. "They are made to look like natural things, carved by wind and rain."

The kors entered the clearing and Zen, Rueez, Char, Jak, and Kon examined the solemn stones. At last, their wonder unquelled, Zen spoke.

"We shall camp here in this glade around this monument. It is a good symbol for us."

"But Zen!" said Jak. "What if the ones who raised these great stones should—"

"Nonsense, Jak! This forest has not stirred in memory, and if it had, the Hunters would have seen it," said Zen. "These are the ancient bones of kors."

"Bones?" asked Rueez.

"Not of kors' body—of this!" Zen tapped his head and snapped his fingers. "Like so, eh? These are from a faraway time of greatness. A greatness we will try to reach ourselves, now."

"But it might be a grave, Zen," said Char.

"Then it is the grave of a great kor, who won't mind our company, after so long."

The 200 families lit fires around the mysterious monument and huddled under hides, eating giss, dried meats and figs and drinking a little of the wine which they had brought in fair quantity.

Guessing at their destiny, they stared at the megaliths and the comet, which climbed the southern sky through the black branches, closer to them now than the night before.

Char and Rueez sat beside the fire with Zen long after the rest were snoozing in the glade and surrounding forest and the flaming star had sunk beneath the southern horizon. "Zen, maybe this was made by bees. Or ants! Great monster ants," Rueez whispered. "They can lift pebbles twice their size, I've seen it with my own eyes. What else could lift these stones?"

"Ha!" Zen slapped his own knee.

"Well," said Char, "how did you know what those strange rocks were? It was no easy thing to know, and yet you came to it easy enough, after we'd only seen two rocks in the ground. You may be wise, Zen, but I'm not stupid. Eh, Hunter?"

Zen nodded respectfully at Char and looked down as he poked a long branch into the embers. "Long ago—when I was a lad under your troop in the far fields, Char—I found something while digging for flint and put it away in my bag." Zen set down the branch and pulled the thin strap of his treasure pouch, which all hunters used to collect precious things they found, over his head. He poured the contents of the small leather pouch into his broad black hand. "Look."

On Zen's palm, Char saw a rounded quartz stone, a green pebble of jade, a nugget of pyrite and even a jagged deep-red ruby. But there was something that caught Char's eye akin to the stones in this glade. It whispered to him from among the shapes—*alive*— unlike the other shapes. It was a disc of gold, pressed flat, its edge scored, its faces depicting scenes of wonder.

"I found this, Char," Zen said. "I hid it. I knew it was something precious from a time when kors did not have to hide things like this. Look at it, Char!"

Char took the gleaming coin and turned it slowly. One side depicted a great house on a mountain built seemingly of stone. The golden drama brought tears to Char's old eyes. On the other side, a kioro and kiori stood holding a child between them. "Who made this beautiful thing?" asked Char, the coin trembling on his old hand.

"I have never known what it meant. But you see it is kors in the gold?" asked Zen. "I knew it must have been from a time long ago when kors were very different."

"Well, Mimu," sighed Rueez.

"Perhaps now you will lead us there," said old Char. He looked into the fire, his face stern as glowing images stirred in his head. He smiled, handing the coin to Zen.

"Zen, are you sad?" asked Rueez.

"I am. If only Win were here."

"And Azurel..." he agreed, and he walked away from the fire to be alone.

Char nodded.

IV

Ez saw the comet over the Hunters Province every night, and every night it was closer.

He heard the child's words louder and louder, though he tried everything to let them die away into the Infinite past: they would not! "The shout lasts no longer on the air than does the whisper," he reminded himself, and yet the whisper screamed inside his head and would not leave. He glanced to the right and left. The others had not seen him. He felt his sin was becoming as visible as the ghost of the boy in the sky.

No, Ez reminded himself, *they are separate, Immurtai and Demurtai. They are opposites. They cannot see by my flesh what is in my soul! Separate, they are separate, still, and always.*

"The Truth will prevail, without those who defy it!"

Ez recited the litany, from memory, startling the other sors.

"The one is nothing compared to the all," he said aloud as the other looked at him askance.

"Brother Turi, you are home. I may talk to you of things that I may not talk to other kors about, I am guessing. Come with me to the bend in the river. No one can hear us speak there." Tor waved a hand in the darkness and led Turi out the back door of their family's home and into the forest.

In the midnight gloom they sat by the river.

Tor looked into his brother's eyes and smiled, but the smile was more formal than felt. "You are an Artist, Turi. You will show the *Demurtai* to the kors for the *Koroshi*. Yours is a toil done inside the hearts of kors."

"Yes, Brother. I value your words. It is the wisdom you have given me that has shown me the Way."

"Soon, the sors will need another sor."

Turi's eyes widened and flashed eagerly, but he did not respond to his brother's statement.

"The sor Ez is dismayed. He is falling into the Immurtai world. He is thirsty, he is hungry, he is lusty; it is seen by all. His struggle is a thorn in the eye of the *Koroshi*, impurifying its vision at a time of peril. It cannot be long before a new sor must be found. And it is most important that this sor be a righteous one, who shall be an example to the common kors, and who will help draw their eyes to the far Truth, again."

"Yes, Brother…" Turi looked at his brother's solemn eyes, which seemed to search the sky's blackness.

"It is not the Way to believe in oneself," Tor said. "To believe in that lie is to deny the True Way. Yet I ask what you believe. I ask you now."

"I believe," said Turi, "that you should be the sor to replace Ez."

"You do." Tor sighed. The tall kor nodded, his shoulders loosening. "It is my duty, then. It is my duty to place myself in this use for the *Koroshi*." Tor bowed his head for a long moment. "A time will come, Brother, when I will ask you to follow me with tools of your making. I will ask you to take these tools and follow me to the Three Stin Cliff. And what I ask you to do then, you must do."

"Brother, I will do it."

Turi nodded and rose.

The brothers left the river together and spoke no more words to each other that night, knowing that they would never have to speak another word to each other in the service of their goal: it was understood.

Azurel woke the next morning, sick and huddled against the wall of the gorge on the dark skulls. The first thing her bleary eyes saw were the small white roots, giss, wedged high between the skulls and bone pebbles by the tide. The strap-basket must have burst when she had fallen into the sea. She collected them, pulling one from the eye socket of an ancient kor and popped it into her mouth.

She sat chewing the refreshing root and looking over the sea. She tasted the salt of its water on the sweet giss. Her fur was stiff and powdered with salt. How had she survived?

She rose. At her sharp movement, dozens of skulls moved away from her. She turned around and looked into the cavern behind her in the daylight.

Azurel stood perfectly still. She lost her breath. She felt like melting ice. The river of bones stretched deeper into the cliff than her eyes could follow. She stared at the skulls around her then. Could this be real? It must be a dream!

At last she forced herself to take another step forward.

A dozen skulls *moved* away at her motion.

She almost fainted, then saw hard crab legs gripping the sand under the jaws of the nearest skull. She ran toward it, and the skull turned and ran, too. She chased it and picked it up.

From its nostrils protruded two long thin eyes like those of a crawfish, and from its eyes, two slender, jointed pincers made hostile gestures. Teeth had been knocked out and four legs on each side jutted between the fused jaws, which sometimes did not match judging from the others in her vicinity. From the hole where the spinal cord emerged curved a fanned tail covered in armor plates.

As Azurel picked up the skull all these appendages tucked in and away, out of sight. She was baffled, relieved, insulted, angered. She threw the skull down. It cracked and revealed the meat of the crab, which, combined with the strong legs and tail, was plentiful. She ate it. Then she slowly walked up over the cracking skulls into the cavern.

The ceiling was a stin above her, curving downward in the distance, and the walls converged, too, as the river of bones rose, disappearing in gloom.

She paused: this place was evil. Her heart pounded. She stared for a long while, stupefied before the bone river. She turned away and faced the shore.

Walking on the soft beach of ground bone she noticed what looked like the body of a dead kor washed high on the pale sand.

Flies swirled as she approached the swollen body. She smelled a foul stench at closer quarters and saw the kor's hands were deformed and bloated into wide paddles. The corpse coughed and barked, suddenly, convulsing its bulk in a corkscrew motion so that its flippers thudded on the wet sand, its head rising twice the height of Azurel and looking down at her with a blubbery face and tiny, blinking eyes. Its nose looked like the barbed pinnacle of the Cinter against the sun as the sea-beast honked a snot-trailed warning.

Azurel ran away down the beach away from the spectacle.

After a while, the sea-beast grunted and waddled down the slope of sand and dove into the waves to swim away.

Azurel sat with her statues in her lap looking at the waves as hours passed. Few dains stirred her desolate mind. She could lie down and die, and join this blanket of skulls, she dained. That was how all of these others had got here. How else could they all come to rest in this place if they had not taken some part? But, why?

"I will find the source of this river," she finally said, aloud, to herself. Her voice bounced back and forth in the distance. It was better than dying without knowing, she dained. And she may find the gate of death—nothing could please her more. Perhaps this was why her life was spared.

Azurel caught herself a crab and she cooked it with a few of the white giss she had retrieved, along with succulent seaweed. She watched the sun sink into the sea as she ate her dinner. And after she slept a deep and dreamless sleep.

When Azurel woke, she found pebbles of flint on the beach and chipped some tools. She made sandals out of the hide of the dead seal she found on the beach and stitched together a leather flask, as well, filling it with water from a spring trickling down the cave's wall.

She sawed cranium bowls off a few skulls with a long elegant saw she had made from a fish's jaw, matching the bowls with cranium lids. Then she braided seaweed to hold a few of these containers together, taking all her remaining giss in one bowl, along with two skull-gourds full of washed crab meat she had cooked.

Thus, she walked back into the cavern.

Stopping at the same point where she had stopped before, she stood still this time and peered into the dying light. This time, she pressed on. Half a stin up the slope of skulls, the cavern's ceiling, barely visible from the light of the huge opening, was only about a quarter-mile high, and the walls of the cavern were only about as wide. The fill of skulls rose a few hundred arms more, then appeared to level out ahead. She pushed on.

Like a shadow, Azurel was erased by the darkness.

As the sound of the waves subsided and the silence fell, the sounds of Azurel's mind reached up to fill the spaces. As the light dimmed, her mind reached out and colored the shadows. She walked through total darkness for another stin and suddenly became paralyzed in the utter night, her legs weak, her feet touching the invisible skulls. Her rasping breath echoed through unseen emptiness. She froze and looked blindly into the infinite blackness. The fear inside her materialized in little chirps and voices whispering on the tunnel's walls. She heard the skulls writhing and chattering around her. There was no way to reach the light and sound that could destroy them, and she fell to her knees.

"Kor!" exploded the thing fused of shadow and fear as it reared its bloated head: "KOR!"

Azurel could barely discern the towering monster that glowed deep purple in the blackness.

"KOR!" it bellowed, swelling before her sightless eyes.

"No," she moaned.

"KOR! KOR!" Its voice splintered off the walls of the tunnel.

"No!" She closed her eyes and held up her arms like the statue Turi had carved.

"NO! NO! NO!" it honked, mocking her.

The beast hurled its layers of blubber toward her and clapped its black flippers. Before it reached her she got up and ran.

"KOR!" the thing shouted, laughing as it crunched the skulls behind her. "You are foolish, KOR!"

Azurel ran at full speed when she struck the wall of the cavern and fell down. She got up and felt along the wall to find her bearings, bleeding over her left eye.

"Wrong way, KOR! Wrong way!" wheezed the waddling beast, grinding the bones behind her.

She ran until she reached the light and only then did the colossal beast vanish behind her.

Bleeding from her collisions, she fell into a stupor on the shore as stars slid over her staring eyes.

In the morning, the hunters were off.

The land dipped into a shallow valley. The forest was lush and thriving though airy and not oppressive. The trees were tall, full and bright with green light, and the forest floor was carpeted in rich spring grasses, dense clover patches, berry brambles and ground crawlers with lavender blossoms. Fat blue snakes slithered through the lush undergrowth and green dragonflies lighted on purple thistles at the bottom of the valley. On the far side of the valley, tall orange toadstools with yellow ruffles sprang up in patches near the roots of ancient trees.

About half way up the far side of the valley, they came across a round slab of stone lying on the grassy slope in a patch of yellow lilies between tall, reaching elms.

Zen stopped then and they all gathered round the curious slab.

Zen banged it with the heavy head of his axe. "It's hollow," he grinned. "Let's lift it. Kon, Rueez, Char, Tuton, Jon, Far, and Hoyt stay. Meanwhile the rest should gather food in the forest."

"Can we lift it, Zen?" asked Tuton.

"Sure!" Kon said.

The kors circled the slab on the sloping field, sizing up the problem as the other kors left to forage—though many of the children sneaked back to watch, and Zen didn't scold them, for he wanted them to remember the things they were seeing now.

The strongest kors grabbed hold of the slab by its upper edge, some wedging pikes and axes beneath the stone. Led by Zen, the hunters hoisted the limestone lid and pushed it over, letting it fall onto the patch of lilies. A humid breath rose from a black well.

In the side of the lid now facing up was a circular frieze. The kors hesitated from entering the thick darkness and looked at the frieze, instead. On the upper two-thirds were carved two curving skeletons, their feet touching at the top, their hands reaching toward a third figure lying in the bottom third. Patches of fur were gone from the third figure and bumps were raised on his body. In the center was the figure of an ancient kor with eyes slitted almost closed and sublime mouth drawn straight in an expression to witness ages by. This central figure had no arms and no legs and a parrot sat on each of his shoulders.

The kors scratched their heads.

"Well, there's only one way to make sense of it," Zen said. "Little Jeeky, since you stayed behind from helping your mother, fetch me a tallow torch from my pack by that little tree."

Jeeky giggled and swung across the trees to the one where Zen had rested his travois. Jeeky opened the flaps and found a tallow torch, which he brought to Zen.

"Good work!" Zen said, pulling the shell-lid from the grease candle and setting it in the field. He struck sparks with his flint and cobble onto straw from the bed of grass and, with a flaming straw, he lit the wick of the tallow torch. He stamped out the burning grass with a broad hand and, sheltering the flame, he walked to the circle of blackness. "Let's go," he said.

Leaning over the hole, he found steep stairs leading down into the earth. He crept down the steps and the air became thick and hot before he emerged in a long level gallery.

Set upon two stone mantles against the long walls on either side were many black alabaster boxes. Zen lifted the polished lid of one of the smaller ones. Lying inside was what Zen believed to be a small cat or ferret wrapped in strips of fine fabric. He opened another, larger box and found a wolf similarly wrapped and preserved. Then he found a parrot, a fennec, a forest dog, an ape—in all 63 assorted animals lay in boxes to either side of the long room.

Zen held the grease candle up to the wall that had known darkness for an amnesia of eons and, engraved in the limestone painted with brilliant colors, was a series of amazing scenes.

In one cunningly carved relief, kors laughed on the side of a rippling lake as purple tigers retrieved birds from reeds on the shore. The kors were taking the fowl from the sky with spears flung with strange curving weapons. The cats brought the birds back to them! Some of the cats wore leashes. Hawks even brought ducks to the kors.

In another relief, a kor rode a large ox-like animal that was pulling a tree-stump out of the ground.

In another, a pack of rare wild dogs attacked a striped bear, and behind the dogs stood kors throwing spears at the angered beast.

A final panel showed a ferocious long-snouted ape solemnly guarding a household while inside kors slept.

All these things these ancient kors could do! Zen was so excited the tallow torch almost went out in his shaking hands. Not only could they put their *Demurtai* into the Immurtai by carving their dreams in stone, but they could even put their *Demurtai* into other creatures, as well! At last he tore away and walked up the stairs to the others, bringing one of the stone coffins in which a parrot had been preserved.

After the others had returned with the rest of the children, they gathered around and marveled at the parrot that had been so painstakingly prepared for its funeral. Then they threw the mummy away and Zen told them what they now knew: kors had built these ancient places.

"How can this be?" said the tall, black-furred Kon, his brow knitted with confusion and fear.

"We know kors have lived in Tai-Raynee for nine millennia," said Char, his pale eyes shining in his gray-furred face. "Before that, no one knows. There are no other kors, nor have there ever been. These monuments must have been built by our fathers and mothers in an age that is now too long ago to remember."

"Yes, Char," Zen grinned. "I can only wonder what else our wise sors have forgotten!"

Zen put the beautiful stone box on his already heavy travois. By this time the baskets were again filled with foods gleaned from the forest and, after eating, the hunter folk embarked, topping the ridge and looking over the next valley.

They had traveled 44 stones, or stins, in the forest. Before them they saw a tall, single megalith covered with moss on the ridge some distance to their left. They saw no other sign of a kor's *Demurtai* anywhere in the small valley before them, so they made out for the next ridge.

They crossed three valleys without spotting more ruins.

It was possible that many had vanished under landslides and advancing growth, pointed out Char—perhaps there were monuments covering these hills at one time. Time could eat even stone, Char reminded them. Yet, when they reached the bottom of the fourth valley, they found something new.

On the far bank of a wide brook was a terraced network of baths carved in yellow alabaster. The kors crossed to the baths over a smooth bridge of yellow stone that was worn and grooved like a natural thing after centuries of use and wind and weather.

The river had been cunningly diverted some distance upstream through a masoned channel and channeled into a pyramidal cascade of round pools. Friezes of swimming and frolicking kioris and kioros were carved in the pool walls overlooking other pools. Protruding from these friezes were finely carved fish heads. Through the mouths of these smiling heads flowed long spouts of water, forced from pools above until, at the bottom, 200 spouts arched into the river from 30 pools.

Although the pools were bearded with fat moss, they were clear-watered and well-circulated, and so all the kors set down their burdens and dove into the baths amidst splashing laughter. They found the water to be hot in some pools and cold in others. Some were steaming and free of moss, others were warm, others cool, and the pool at the top of the cascade was icy cold. Old Char deemed that there must be springs underneath the baths. Ice-cold spouts fell into fire-hot baths, and steaming spouts fell into frigid pools, and every combination between. Rueez climbed onto the wide wall of the highest pool and jumped from one pool to the next, finally belly-flopping in the river as the children screamed and giggled.

The kors lounged on the walls of the pools in the sun, making love, admiring the murals and talking as the children splashed tirelessly in the water.

Rueez journeyed up river to stand guard, alone.

A careless troop of white baboons swung in the trees over the sunning kors on their way to the river. Little Jeek and some other boys and girls leaped down from the treetops into the pools with little squeals.

Zen stood and roared at the apes above and they quickly dispersed, heading downstream. Zen remembered the murals he had seen in the strange tomb after the baboons had gone.

They ate a late lunch and shouldered their packs, clean, refreshed and good-humored as they climbed the other side of the valley through sparse woods in the long shadows of afternoon. About halfway up the ridge, the slope became gentler, and the trees thinned away into a field. Across the field, at the top of the ridge, stood a giant white kor.

The kors were first alarmed, then thrilled—for it was merely a statue at least a hundred hands tall, standing on the crest of the ridge. The marble colossus was imposingly muscled, his arms bent and his hands spread symmetrically on his chest; he looked expansively over the valley, facing north, more or less toward Tai-Raynee. A large chunk had been knocked from his face by the artless hand of time. Other than this, the statue may have been raised a day ago.

"It's like Azurel's statue of Win," said Sannava.

"Yes," Zen smiled. "Azurel should be here, by thunder! This is where she belongs, even more than the rest of us."

Rueez looked sadly at the distances they had crossed.

As they approached the statue, fascinated by its size and beauty, Zen had the party camp in the field at its feet to forage food. Tearing his eyes away, Zen left with a hunting party to find game.

By nighttime their stomachs and their baskets were full again, and they were hard at work with the hides and the leftover meat and bones and grease from the deer they managed to bag. The colossus, purple against the starry sky, smiled over them at the top of the ridge as they worked.

When they made use of what they could of the deer, they discarded the remains in the forest.

Then they slept. They had journeyed 49 stins from Tai-Raynee.

After breakfast and a careful repacking of the camp they moved up the field to the top of the ridge at the feet of the statue.

Below, they saw a deep valley.

That valley was filled by the temples and ziggurats of a city.

V

A network of reflecting ponds and fountains still circulated through overgrown parks and monuments, all powered by water rushing from an overgrown dam barely visible at the northeastern end of the valley.

Billowing waterfalls poured from tunnels in the solid granite dam and filled the double trough of a great aqueduct arching down the valley to the side of the ziggurat to their left. A white cataract of water bounded down the steps from the side of the ziggurat that faced the city.

The ziggurat was composed of three superimposed pyramids built of granite blocks. A square tower with many open floors stood on the twelve corners of its steps. One of these stone towers had half collapsed, but the others were still solid, with trees growing on their floors. Broad causeways linked the four outer towers to four towers on the first step of the pyramid. Causeways linked these to four smaller towers on the corners of the second step. The pinnacles of these innermost towers rose 90 hands over the top of the ziggurat.

Overlooking the city, an ornate stone building sat in the middle of the high courtyard on top of the pyramid and on its roof stood another great statue like the one they stood beside, this one looking east toward the dam.

On the side of the ziggurat facing the city water flowed down into a rectangular lake bordered by tall trees with bare trunks crowned by glossy fronds. Beside the lake was a great stone maze, a jungle of corridors exactly the size and shape of the lake. To the right of this, on the southwest end of the valley, stood a ziggurat like the one on the left. On the building at its summit stood another colossus, this one looking west.

Many beautiful buildings bordered the reservoir and the maze, and on the terraced hills below and on the other side of the valley they could see overgrown dwellings, temples, and monuments. On the top of the ridge across from them they saw the back of another colossus, looking south.

"Daddy!" laughed Jeeky, leaping onto his father's head. "What is it?"

Kon looked at Zen. "Home, Jeek."

Zen smiled and nodded.

Zen told them all to meet at dusk atop the ziggurat that spewed water. Agreeing, they split up to explore, stopping in little temples or shrines and discovering fountains and patios and homes as they made their way down the side of the valley.

Rueez and old Char accompanied Zen as he headed toward the heart of the city on the floor of the valley.

"How did we lose this?" asked old Char, subdued.

"That is the question we must answer," nodded Zen. "Perhaps this place will tell us."

They left their travois on the ground floor of a tower at the corner of the ziggurat of flowing water. Inside the tower, they found a heavy stone staircase, and, casting wide eyes at each other, they climbed to the second story.

Char noticed the tower was built of stones cut to balance one another in an easy pattern of ascent. A graceful agreement of weights seamed the pillars of these monuments; the irregular stones seemed to have already cracked and compressed together, at rest though not in ruin.

There were no walls on any of the floors of the towers. Four massive columns standing twenty hands tall rose at each corner of the polished floors. On each floor, an inner circle of pillars supported a domed ceiling of cantilevered rings of stone, which in turn supported the center of the floor above.

They reached the third story, and from there the causeway crossed the first step of the ziggurat. To either side, the ramp was covered with ancient wind-stirred trees. They crossed the causeway, entered the next tower, and climbed three stories to the next causeway on the second step to the third tower. Again, they climbed three floors and crossed the causeway, this time to the top of the ziggurat.

"Ah! So beautiful!" said Zen, and he breathed deeply and pounded the snow-white galaxy on his chest. His teeth flashed in the sun.

Rueez and Char looked with him from the ziggurat over the valley. Eleven towers with their square cantilevered pinnacles rose around them. Green parrots sat in the belfries and circled around the pinnacles.

The waterfall issued from a wide tunnel below, spilling over the second and first steps of the pyramid, the creamy waters joining the long lake.

The lake was mirrored by the maze and the other ziggurat in perfect symmetry.

Behind them, on top of the courtyard's central temple, stood the white colossus, looking out over the swashing aqueduct and the distant dam to the north.

They approached this temple now and saw that carved into its outer walls were profiles of kors, layered one-beneath-the-other, wrapping the building. The first figure, fully exposed, was a small hunched kor with a rounded muzzle. He wore a robe and bore a curved crown.

As the figures marched forward, with profiles laid one behind the other, they grew taller and more handsome, and the expression on their faces changed from fierce sneers to kind smiles. By the third wall they were wearing capes and crowns and by the fourth wall they held scepters of amazing craft in their hands.

Then, suddenly, the procession of kor kings became more austere and the last two wore no robes and their faces were serious and expressionless, and the rest of the fourth wall was taken up by a carving of a kor Zen and the others recognized from the lid of the tomb they found in the forest. It was an armless and legless kor who sat grim-faced, eyes closed, with parrots on his shoulders. Parrots flew to his right toward a great stone on a high plain. The stone, though of a slightly different pinnacle, was immediately recognizable as the Cinter, and the plain that rose above the Cinter in the distance, Tai-Raynee.

"Could this be Sor?" Zen asked.

Char rubbed his chin. "The Sor?"

"Of course," said Rueez, "it was Sor who told them all to leave this place."

"Now, Rueez," said Zen, "things could not be so simple." Zen gestured at their surroundings. "They would not leave because he told them to."

They went inside the building through a door on the corner between the first and last walls. They saw twilit murals carved inside. On the wall that blocked the dam, an intricate mural depicted the dam's construction and the building of the aqueduct. On the frieze to the right was a rendering of a great terraced palace on a mountain, like the one on Zen's coin. On the wall facing the city was a plan of the maze, worn away at one corner. On the northwest wall was a carving of the great lake and Tai-Raynee beyond it with the Cinter rising in the distance.

"What's this?" Zen grunted. In this last frieze, many kioris and kioros stood on broad-sailed barges which were being loaded at docks on the great lake. Piled on the decks were barrels and crates and the corpses of kors, folded ceremoniously. These barges sailed upriver to Tai-Raynee, while other processions traveled overland, entering the ancient cave at the base of the Cinter. The three kors looked at each other, baffled.

"This must have something to do with why they left," said old Char. "Perhaps some great tragedy drove them to Tai-Raynee, and they bore their dead with them to bury in the new land."

"You may well be right, Char," Zen said. He rubbed his beard.

"The Truth is in Tai-Raynee, old parrot! Tai-Rayneeee!"

The three wheeled as green feathers fluttered past them into the room.

Furious, Zen leaped at the parrot, backing it into a corner. "What did you say, bird!" He grabbed it, and it squawked a long, anguished cry in his fingers.

"Zen, it is a witless bird!" cried gray Char.

"A witless bird, you say? Didn't you hear it speak?" Zen kept a cruel grip on the screaming, flapping creature.

"I have heard them speak before, Zen! A friend of my grandfather taught a green parrot to say things," Char said.

"These words may be ancient," Rueez said. "The birds may have repeated them for generations.

"And they live a very long time," Char said.

Zen looked at the bird, which gnawed his hand. He turned and walked out into the sunlight on the courtyard, holding the bird high. The others followed.

The parrot squawked, and others circled testily in the air around the towers as Zen looked up at them. They swooped above the courtyard, jabbering and cawing. "Many truths, many truths!" one said.

"Plague! Plague! Plague!" cried another.

"The Truth is in Tai-Raynee!" screeched another.

The words echoed down to them from the measureless past.

"The secret of Sor!"

"Koroshi, Raaaaak! Raaaaak!"

"Only, only, only!"

"Only Truth, *raaaaak!"*

"Go, you must! Go, you must!"

"Tai-Raynee, old parrot."

"Truth! Truth! Truth!"

"Plague! Plague! Plague!"

"Forever Truth! *Raaaak!"*

Char remembered the mural and the half-kor with parrots on his shoulders. "Are these the words of Sor himself?" he asked, laughing in wonder. "They tell the story, Zen!"

"That they do," said Zen, half-convinced and half-amazed to find such an easy answer to the mystery. "That they do."

As the green sky dimmed, the families met on the broad courtyard atop the citadel of flowing water.

Zen climbed to the roof of the building there, and standing at the feet of the colossus, he spoke to them.

"Hunters! Our new home!" He spread his arms.

They all cheered, their eyes bright as they stood together on the ziggurat. Zen smiled and brought together his hands. "Hunters, we should build tables on this courtyard that overlooks our home, and let us install this artfully carved building with a kitchen and then build fire-pits so that when we all have cause for celebration, we may sit up here and dine and dance. But for now, all of those who agree we have something to celebrate should send one of their sons to gather wood in the twilight and we shall roast the deer that remains from yesterday upon this mighty pyramid."

The kioris and kioros laughed warmly and sent out their sons who ran springing down the ramparts and towers laughing as the young kioris stared excitedly after them, wanting to go with them, but the adults wanted firewood to actually make it back to the temple some time this evening.

"For the most important part," said Zen, "we must determine meeting places. We must use one of these structures that is best suited for a tannery, and find places where there is clay. All those kors who were crafters in Tai-Raynee must set about finding the provisions they will need for their craft. They should take one of the buildings by the lake which is best suited to sheltering their tools and all the Immurtai they will need and lay out their site. Then we must build a kiln for the crafters.

"As for the rest of us, we hunters should work to clear away the roads as we hunt and build up stock. Each should take the wood he has cleared from the streets and use it for his own home. Plant as much giss as you can and trade it for other goods with kors. No one will stop you but nature herself, and no one will force you but your own heart. If a kor tricks another, or hurts another, that kor shall pay the same he has taken from another. That is the law so you can be free, like the birds in the sky!

"Choose any place for your home, hunters, except for these two great monuments." Zen pointed at the other ziggurat. "Many of you will want to choose other stone buildings for your homes, and these should go to the first families who claim them. But do not choose hastily. There are very many and some more beautiful than others. Dain of what you want your home to be, of where you want it to be and also how you want it to be, and do not compromise your comfort because of a building's beauty. Do everything for your own happiness now with both wisdom and desire. Do not be afraid that you will be shunned for your decision, especially if it is grand! We are not in Tai-Raynee any longer, Hunters! Build your homes exactly to your liking, and we shall all hope for your success!

"It shall now be law that Hunters are free." Zen looked at Jak and Kon and Char and Rueez and some of the other great hunters now. "It is like being away on the 'Far Fields' again, eh Hunters? Free to dain of the Other Ways! Only now there is no Tai-Raynee to return to, and we are home! And if loving this place of ours is Immurtai," said Zen, looking at the festooned towers in the sky around them, "let us call this place Immurtia!"

And the people agreed, and feasted that night, their singing clear and high on the violet sky. They toasted Zen and made him their chief because he was wise and good and loved them. And they celebrated freedom.

Anto and Sannava stole away and climbed to the top floor of one of the towers. And in that shadowed loft encompassed by stars Anto entered Sannava beneath him at last. He rocked slowly, the wind whipping through the pillars, and the heavens around them moaned and tilted as they kissed the breath out of each other afloat amid the burning stars.

Zen and Neon walked through the Hunters, who were gathered around the fires on the citadel and asked them about the things they had seen that day.

Some found monuments filled with animals similar to the one they found earlier. On the lids of these chambers were carved the same mysterious design, two skeletons over an ill kor. The black alabaster coffins were being emptied and cleaned so they might be used to store food and wares.

Zen learned about many bright temples in the city and a few small, dark ones. In the open, pillared temples, some found central fountains still burbling, surrounded by wonderful statues. The statues depicted strong kioros and kioris smiling, a musk ox, a giant giss root and other queer vegetables, a fish, a block of stone on which was carved fire, a huge wheel and a giant cluster of grain. One saw a crawfish, and other similar stone idols carved with healthy, buxom symmetry. Zen remarked that these temples sounded like an excellent place for a party.

In the smaller temples, which were closed and dark, were solemn murals and gold statues of the thin, limbless kor. One of these temples, the largest of its kind, had only a boulder of several tons sculpted into the shape of a skull in the center of its floor. Inside this temple, Zen was told the carved symbol with the two skeletons and the strange half-kor gleaming dimly in the center of its domed ceiling.

After conferring long into the night with Char and Jak and Rueez, Zen concluded that nine millennia ago, plague must have stricken the ancient kors, and persuaded by the prophet Sor, they left the city to live in Tai-Raynee. The despairing words the parrots echoed were the only explanation for the tombs and the grim imagery in the temples. That their ancient ancestors left so much behind, however, and never retrieved or even recreated the miracles of this city, did not make sense to Zen. Perhaps the plague had taken too many and the survivors were broken by the tragedy. Zen frowned, unable to understand why the ancient kors would choose to live in Tai-Raynee.

"The truth is in Tai-Raynee, *raaaaak!*"

Zen threw a hot ember at the swooping parrot, shrugging off his puzzlement. It really didn't matter, he dained.

Putting to rest the riddle of history, Zen set his mind on the future, and his dreams were bounteous that night after Neon made love to him on the highest floor of the northernmost tower, the comet framed between black pillars, closer, again, than the night before.

Zen and the rest of the kors had agreed to meet on the ziggurat at dusk to discuss where the crafters would set up their shop, where the hunters would base their tannery, and where the houses for stock should be.

The hunters hunted till late afternoon, when they found themselves at a large, pillared building on the south bank of the lake. A field lay between it and the shore. Noting that it was not far from the site the crafters were establishing, they chose it for the tannery. The crafters busily collected reeds from the lake and wove baskets, sinking them in the lake after they were woven and lining them to dry and shrink in the sun on the part of the granite edge that they had weeded and washed.

Meanwhile, beside the crafters, the hunters butchered the deer and fowl and fish and two white boar they had bagged that day. They had hunted down the river, which flowed in a square moat around the southern ziggurat and fell off a cliff into a pool that fed a wide, slow river in the valley below the city. They found this valley was rich with game, and some banks of the river bore clay suitable for earthenware. Char had even found a deposit of flint at the foot of the cliff. They hauled a sample of the clay and a load of flint back with their prey up a broad ancient stairway made of hard stone. Some youngsters were dispatched to take it over to the crafters, who were pleased with their quality and set about gathering more.

The hearthkeepers had not stayed idle, either. The wives of the hunters with their army of children gathered great quantities of nuts and figs and fruits from the forest. Between the crafters and the ziggurat of flowing water, the hearthkeepers found a broad field, scattered with trees and many stone houses overlooking the lake. In each house, they stored one kind of food in their few baskets and in the small alabaster coffins they had salvaged from the tombs and washed with boiling water. They sorted grains and certain giss into piles on the stone floors, which they also washed with boiling water. They enlisted the children to weed and wash the outside of the buildings and the surrounding grounds.

Since it was spring and the forest had not been foraged, they were able to stock ahead a few days. Kon and his troop astounded everyone with their harvest of game, a whole herd of Green Moose, and kept the tanners and hearthkeepers busy curing and smoking the surplus meat. Yet they worked so fast they were able to go out with their daughters and their children to search for homes that day.

At dusk, all gathered atop the ziggurat to feast and discuss the things they had learned and accomplished. Zen told the crafters which tools they would need most, and the crafters told Zen what materials they would need to make them. The kiln would require a few large stones that the crafters could not set alone.

Neon told Zen that the children found a building in which were piled axe heads and spearheads made from some strange rock like the disc Zen found. He brought it to the attention of the others and made it a priority for the crafters to look into it.

Then, afterwards, the wives spoke to their husbands about the homes they had found before settling into sleep upon the ziggurat of flowing water.

The next day the hunters agreed there was enough meat in the storehouses for them to go with their wives while their sons set about tanning the skins and curing the meats. They walked arm-in-arm through the forested hills to choose their homes.

After checking in on the work at the tannery, Zen went with Neon to the place of the crafters. He asked Kem, Kon's son, if he had any luck with the axe and spearheads. To his delight, Kem ran back to the long-pillared building the crafters had chosen and emerged a few moments later with an axe for Zen. Kem had managed, with a grinding wheel one of the crafters made, to scrape the green from the outside and sharpen the blade. He mounted the heavy golden head on a thick hardwood handle, binding it with boiled sap, strips of hide, and carefully fitted wooden wedges. It was a beautiful instrument, and an elated Zen weighed its balance. "Can the rest be fitted out this way?" he asked.

"Yes, they're made of hard stuff!" said Kem, shaking his head as though he had had a stubborn fight with the metal. "They are in good shape! The hearthkeepers found many, of all different sizes."

"Marvelous," said Zen. "What do you call it?"

"This stuff? I haven't, Zen!"

"Dain a name."

Kem's brow worked. Dain was a difficult word, a new word, and it meant something hidden away and never seen. Azurel called her words 'tools,' just like her other tools. But to make tools she must act—to make words she must dain. It was the same, she said. Hunters had quickly understood and approved of her word, and they used it more and more as they met the challenges of their new life. Kem dained a new word for this hard bright stuff they had found: "Beetleback!"

"Good!" Zen said. "I know the beetles you mean. See that every family can have a beetleback axe and let them trade lumber and other goods for them. You crafters should do well here, I think! Let each crafter trade his tools for other goods. The best crafters shall benefit from their work so other crafters will always try harder and find better new ways. That way, everyone will have better tools, eh, Char? And crafters will eat better food, too," Zen winked. "We must really learn these ancient crafts, Kem. Tomorrow we will build you a kiln." Zen bid goodbye to the crafters and congratulated them on their fine work. Then he and Neon then walked along the square lake.

Neon took Zen's arm and laughed, looking into her husband's blue eyes. "Zen, I know the place we should choose," she winked.

Zen looked into her violet eyes and laughed, yielding to her pull.

She led Zen up a winding path to a shady, overgrown place with a wide outcrop of mossy stone overlooking the ziggurat of flowing water. Zen stood acrest the outcrop, holding Neon's hand. The trees growing among the ruins behind them were sweet green and full of fiery red flowers above that smelled of cinnamon and honey. Zen smiled.

All that was left on this patch of ground was a stone wall and some pillars. In the wall was a fireplace and chimney, carved deep with forest and animal images. The wall was 25-hands-tall, as were the two rows of rock columns beside the buried floor. Forest scenes were carved on these pillars, both frightening and amusing: harts and foxes, tigers and snails, boars and butterflies, kioris and kioros leaping through artful trees.

"This will be the hearth of the Feast Hall, and the rest of the house will be over there, behind," he said, waving an arm, "with windows that look down over this valley."

"And did you see our fountain?" Neon pointed. "It's overgrown, but a little trickle of water still squeezes out. If we cleaned it, it would spray into the air again. Imagine, Zen, our own water!"

Zen walked to the fountain at the edge of the dark outcrop and looked over the valley at the ziggurat. "There is a road beneath this cliff that leads past other homes and into Immurtia. We must dig out that road and weed it clean so we have easy passage to the meeting places."

"Zen! Are you not excited about the house?"

He turned to her and grabbed her, lifting her up. "Yes!" he boomed, then set her down and planted a huge kiss on her beautiful kiori mouth. "And we will begin building today!"

Neon laughed as Zen ran to the fireplace and started swinging his new axe into a tree trunk. The blade rang as it sliced through wood again after eons of sleep.

Neon worked in the garden, cleaning the fountain of choking moss and dirt and digging out the courtyard of stone tiles.

Zen sang as he felled trees behind her.

Similar sounds echoed through the hills around them.

That night they all met on the ziggurat again.

They ate and talked about the homes they had found and discussed clearing the roads.

Zen saw Sara sitting by one of the fires.

Sannava had left with Anto, and Tuton was away with Kon's family.

Zen went to Sara and sat beside her. "We all miss Win, but not so much as you, Sara." He took her hand. "You of course will stay with us, for we're your family now."

"No, Zen. I cannot burden you with Tuton and Sannava and me. Win would have never had such a thing!"

"But Mother!" laughed Sannava as she and Anto approached. She was looking at Anto and smiling. "Anto and I are husband and wife."

"Oh!" said Zen.

"We just agreed," said young Anto.

"Oh, Sannava, I am so happy for you!" Sara hugged her daughter and Anto.

"Marvelous, my boy!" Zen said, slapping Anto's back stoutly. "You'll be a good husband!"

"We found a little house by the lake, and we are going to prepare it immediately," said Anto. He suddenly rolled his eyes and grinned. "We will have much to do and remember."

"Well, if you need any help putting things right, just ask!" Zen said.

"No, Mimu. I won't need any help. My wife and I will do very well, all right!" Anto squeezed Sannava's hand confidently, looking into her eyes.

"I'm sure you will, Anto," smiled Sara. "Still, just ask."

"Grandfather Char promised to talk to me about the household," said Anto.

"That is good," Zen nodded. "Bounty to you both. I'll spread this news!" He looked at Sara. "Well, Sara, then it's final. You and Tuton are going to stay with us from now on as family. I will not have it any other way for my friend Win."

"No, Mimu!" said Tuton, who approached the fire, grinning from ear to ear. A big-boned and still clumsy youth, Tuton was almost as tall as Zen and even broader, and well on his way to becoming a champion hunter, like his father. His arm was around the tall, black-furred daughter of Kon. "Seenay and I are married tonight, and we have found a beautiful house with five rooms and windows and a terrace for a garden with a stone fence. And Mother will be staying with us in our new home! She'll even have her own cottage!"

Sara protested, but the tall and beautiful Seenay smiled at her young husband's exuberance and nodded at Sara, assuring her that she willed it also. And so Sara agreed and thanked Zen as she wept tears of joy for her children.

"All the world is getting married!" Zen said, congratulating Tuton. "That is good, for we will have many little kors running around soon." He kissed Sara as he bid goodbye and left to find his sons and talk to them about building the feast hall and the house before they got themselves married, too.

Rueez sat on the edge of the ziggurat, only a tear betraying his grief as he looked at the city. Unable to imagine her dead, his fear for Azurel only grew as he wondered what sad path she had taken, unaware that they had found a world where they could finally live unbroken.

Twenty days had passed. Azurel sat on the beach, staring at a skull in which a crab had made its home.

It was a marvelous thing that a creature could be shaped so perfectly to fill the skull of a kor. It was obvious that the death of a kor must have preceded the life of this odd creature. Life molded itself, Azurel dained. It perfected its shape, like an artist, over time.

In the days since she entered the blackness, she had puttered along the shore, turning up shells and collecting them, building an altar of skulls and sea conches, and she set her statues on top of it.

She found a perfect chunk of green jade washed ashore on one of her morning walks. It might have fallen out of the cliff above. It was smaller than the pieces her father found for her statues, but Azurel could see a kor child's soft limbs in its translucent heart. She began to work the stone with improvised tools.

She pretended the pit of fear and insanity twisting into the world behind her did not exist. Once or twice her eyes were drawn into it, and she could feel the beast watching her inside the distant gloom, always. But she knew it would not advance into light and that it would not shout into sound and that she was safe on the bright shore with the rasping waves.

The beach was long and she did not feel too confined. She established a home base at one end and found a daining rock on the other end high up on the cliff overlooking the sea.

The tunnel waited.

She could not go in.

The horror was limitless, there.

She looked at the sun and the crabs and the skulls, working on the statue of a kor child as the tides washed her days away.

VI

It was dusk on the Fifth Day as Ez stared at the ghost in the southern sky.

Tonight the sors were to take the black giss and make the long comet loop into the far reaches so the pure light of the *Demurtai* could gather them in, only to be betrayed, atom by atom, back into the Immurtai world of flesh and dirt and wood and water.

Ez feared which world he would choose each time he took the dark giss roots. Tonight he feared he was lost. The oneness, the answer, the Truth, was breaking down into the many bright things of the world that he could no longer seem to ignore.

That night he wept, and all the sors saw him.

Tor placed three black giss in his hand.

Ez saw that his roots had come from a different bowl. He chewed and swallowed them without expression, and his fellow sors watched as he lay down and died: his only possible penance.

"Turi, wake up. I must speak to you."

Turi rose, and the brothers went out to sit together by the bend in the chattering river.

"What is it, Brother?" asked Turi.

"I have been chosen."

Turi's breath fell. "Yes?"

"And it is time you know some Truths." Tor sat with his legs crossed and his arms hanging loose. His eyes were closed.

Turi listened to the kor who had become more than his brother. Tor had merged with the *Koroshi*. He was holy now, and Turi looked at him with not a little fear. "Tell me these things so we both know the Truth," whispered the young Artist.

"The importance of the Artist is that he acts without any self," said Tor. "He makes objects for no other reason but to demonstrate that. What offends him he must create as his duty, what hurts his own heart he must create as his capitulation. He gives up his own Immurtai dreams, but in return gains power over the *Demurtai* of all kors, and becomes one with the *Demurtai*, one with the *Koroshi*, one with Eternity, one with Truth."

"Yes, Brother." Turi nodded. "Go on."

"The power of the sor is that his self is without any action. He gives up his own body, yet in return the sor gains power over all the Immurtai. Do you see?"

"Your words shine a new light."

"The sor Ez is dead."

"More life to the *Koroshi*!" Turi said.

"Yes. And tonight is the night I ask you to come with me to bring your tools for the hacking and for the cutting. Tonight I ask you to do what you promised."

"What is that, Brother?"

"If you do not do it you will be struck down and forgotten to the *Koroshi*," said Tor. There was no expression in his voice or face, and yet the words stabbed Turi like icicles.

"What is it?" Turi murmured.

"You must tie my arms and legs to the field on the cliff by the Sea of the *Koroshi*. I will eat ten black giss and you will cut my arms from my body. Then you will cut my legs from my body. And my ears. And my testicles. I will be your work of art, Brother. You will have made the perfect work of art, Immurtai without *Demurtai*. And I—I will be the perfect sor, *Demurtai* without Immurtai. I have been chosen to save the *Koroshi*. You have been chosen to help me. The evil in the sky will vanish then, and peace will be restored to the *Koroshi*."

Turi wept and covered his face.

Tor ignored his tears. "Now, let us depart."

Turi sobbed as he tied the body of his tall, strong brother to the grass of that highest field three nights after they had left for the great cliff. And indeed the flaming ghost in the sky did not appear that night, as his brother had predicted.

"Do not weep, Turi," Tor said. "Just do."

Turi stifled his tears and pulled the knots tight. He chose an axe as his brother chewed the ninth giss.

"When we do this we deny the *Demurtai* a place in the Immurtai and the Immurtai a place in the *Demurtai*. If any connection is made between them, the *Koroshi* is corrupted as sure as the flesh that tries to attach to it, and the Amoli is mocked by the lies of mud and wind and wood."

Turi listened in wordless fear. Tor was not his brother anymore and it confused him.

"Give me the tenth root," Tor said, seeing beyond the black heavens.

Turi placed the root in his mouth and turned away to look at the sea, black and etched with purple, three stins below. He wept in fear.

"It is time," whispered Tor, startling him. "Take your tool."

Turi lifted his tool, a fine sharp knife Azurel had made, and without expression he proceeded to cut off the arms of Tor. How can I fear him so? Turi asked himself. I am killing him! He is helpless and I am destroying him! Why do I fear him so?

His brother did not move his limbs, except to improve access for the cutting tools, until the dark work was finished.

Turi sewed up each wound so his brother might survive the night.

And then, after an hour had passed, Tor suddenly sat up with a sickening motion of his torso. He stared at the starlit sea. "You are the greatest Artist who has ever lived, Brother," said Tor.

Turi gasped. Only now could he see it. His brother was now the most powerful kor in Tai-Raynee.

Tor

Turi dragged Tor on a travois back to Tai-Raynee, and took him before the sors inside the cave, and they fell prostrate before him, as Turi had foreseen.

VII

"Here, little crabby-wabby," said Azurel, jiggling the orange flesh of a mussel. She threw the meat at the scrambling creature, which pinched it up precisely. "That's a good boy, Rueez." She stroked his head.

She called another skull-crab Sannava, a light, fragile-lined skull with seaweed hair, and another she named little Erg, a baby's skull with big wide eyes, and another she named Zen, a black, stout skull with full teeth, big canines, deep eyes and a strangely noble presence.

Azurel started her melancholy naming game as a grim reminder of her loved ones. It was a sarcastic gesture, a lewd proposal to replace them as one might replace any other thing. Only when she could see her own face in one of the skull-crabs and almost named it "Azurel" did the game become too perverse. She settled with the dozen or so crabs she had already named and left it at that.

"Come here, Sannava," said Azurel.

The pretty skull-crab with its elegant features waddled toward the meat in her hand.

With a *crunch!* Azurel sent a heavy stone through the cranium, killing the crab. Then she separated the organs from the meat for her lunch.

How interchangeable are we kors, she dained as she washed the meat in the green sea and threw away the bits of skull. The sors believed that. She hailed their great wisdom in this dark place where it was so comical, this place with millions of eyes and none of them seeing, millions of skulls and none of them daining.

She finished her lunch and ran down the beach. The sea glistened. Skulls rattled and rolled over the sand as the waves pushed and dragged. She splashed through the foam and spotted a skull that she recognized.

"Ho, Zen!" She hailed him, waving her arm. Scrambling upright was the crab Zen, his confident, alert face warming Azurel's heart for a moment. "It's out to sea again for you," she laughed, hoisting the skull and lobbing it out into the ocean, where it promptly sank. She sat down and waited for Zen to emerge. She enjoyed watching Zen's murky image climbing through the green shelves of water and finally glistening round in the sun. He did just that, again, and she tossed him a piece of Sannava's meat, which he eagerly ate.

Azurel cast her eyes over the sea. She felt a stirring anger or eagerness inside her, and she puzzled as she looked at the horizon and the faded chalk cliffs across the sea. What was wrong? What was she feeling? What was she daining? She didn't know.

She walked along the stripe of sticky foam looking over the shells and other surprises the sea presented each morning. She felt the cave that covered half her world like a perpetual night breathing its cold breath on her shoulders.

She saw a large group of crabs ahead. She went to investigate and scared them away. They scrambled down to the water, revealing the swollen leg of a large kor. Two arms and another leg were strewn nearby.

She knelt, vomiting into the sea surging around her.

She felt the growing warmth in her belly and clutched the unfinished kor child carved in jade on a leather cord around her neck.

Azurel looked into the blackness where all her fears waited for her.

Zen and the others worked on their homes and on the roads which connected them to the center of Immurtia.

A good kiln was built for the crafters who made pottery of new and original designs, designs that had hidden in their hearts for years before they came to Immurtia. In a few weeks, the tannery was fitted out, the crafting place was stocked and Immurtai sources established, and the food stocks were bounteous, well ordered, and secure. The kors continued to clear the roads and monuments with beetleback axes and saws.

During these weeks, Zen and his family accomplished many things. Zen and his sons worked on clearing the road below their home. They pulled out the tree stumps and dug down to the heavy cobblestones with their newly-found shovel-blades made of the beetleback, and they set the hexagonal cobbles straight and washed them with water from the spraying fountain which Neon had cleaned.

They used the trees they felled to build Zen's hall. Zen wanted the hall to be strong like the ruins it was built on, so he dained of an 'other way' he could build it with wood that would be nearly as strong as stone. He wished they could work with stone as well as the previous occupants of the hall, but until they learned more, it was not possible.

Neon and two of her sons dug out the stone floor of the hall, chopping at the roots of the tree stumps with their new spades and stone hand axes as Zen and his sons stripped trees down to logs. They obtained another of the metal axes from the crafters, who continued to scour the city for artifacts. These mighty instruments had given Zen an inspiration.

He and his sons dug a U-shaped trench around the hall with the stone wall and chimney filling the gap in the 'U.' They measured, cut, and laid the first logs in the trench, then hacked grooves into their upper surfaces. The ends of the logs were notched and interwoven with each other at the corners of the hall and sealed with boiled sap.

Log after log, they raised sturdy walls against the stone pillars, and when the job was done, Zen and Neon and their four sons stood back and looked at the handsome, even-lined hall. Sweating in the afternoon sun and laughing as the wind cooled and tickled their weary bodies, they admired their handiwork.

Zen and his boys planted tall logs in the ground opposite the pillars against the walls, founding each of them deep in the ground.

When this was done they climbed on the walls and hoisted heavy logs into place over the stone pillars. The stone pillars had pegs on top to which they had matched notches on the beams. His sons lashed in a tight network of cross-branches and poured boiled sap over all the joints in the framework of the roof before laying large, thickly-woven mats of reed over the roof, followed by broad hide patchworks from the deer and antelope and sloth which Zen and his sons had downed. The roof was slightly pitched toward the valley to allow the heavy rains of winter to drain into the gutter they had dug out in the courtyard.

Jeek Pulled a Weed

The hall was completed before the house, and the family lived in it, sleeping by the fireplace with its dreaming stone, until they finished the other rooms. They built furniture, cleaned the garden, and planted it with red and brown giss, which the Hearthkeepers found growing naturally in parts of the forest.

Every night the kors met at dusk atop the ziggurat to dine, to discuss progress, and to sleep. However, as the kioris and kioros settled their homes and smoothed the edges of their new industry, they became more spread out, and Zen deemed the time had come to meet in the mornings at the new tannery and that only one of the kioris and kioros in charge of households need come. He also declared that feasts on the ziggurat would be reserved for holidays that they would name later. Then at the meeting the next morning, he decreed it to be the First Day, and thereby weeks, and most importantly Fifth Days, were reinstated.

The comet, the great ghost that had wandered so close, wandered away by the time their first Fifth Day had come around.

VIII

On the First Day after the comet disappeared, Zen was accosted by many kors as he returned to the tannery with his new troop after hunting below the city on the banks of the river.

"Mimu!" said Jak. "My little Jeek is caught in the maze of stone!"

"Oh?" said Zen, lowering his travois, upon which was lashed one red elk, from his shoulders. "How long has he been stuck, then?" he laughed.

"Two days."

Zen scowled. "What! Why hasn't anyone got him out?"

"We have tried, Mimu," said Kon's wife, Buri. "We sent many after him, all lost. My husband, too!"

"You mean Kon can't find his way out?" Zen laughed, slapping his leg.

"Fifty kors have gone into the place, Mimu, one after the other, and all are lost," said Jak.

Zen's face became grave. "It's a tangled course?"

"It's a trap," Jak said.

"From what Kon shouted out to us, the walls are ingeniously tangled."

"Yes, there is a plan of it in the temple of flowing water. We should be able to find them."

"We checked it, Mimu. One corner of the map is worn away, and it ruins it."

Zen rubbed his beard. "Well, take me to this trap."

They led Zen to the entrance.

The maze was a quarter-stin long and an eighth-stin wide. Its dark walls were three kors tall. Its straight outer walls surrounded a confusing network of corridors.

There was no ceiling, so twilight lit the halls. The entrance was a simple gap in the outer wall, within which was a complicated intersection of passageways. On the outer wall and on the inner walls Zen noticed deep reliefs showing various scenes.

Zen had wanted to investigate the carvings in the dark labyrinth more thoroughly before but was always busy with more pressing matters. Now it was the most pressing matter, and Zen paused at its door.

The Maze

An overhang of stone prevented the walls from being scaled and had no doubt helped preserve the carvings. The tops of the walls were studded with bronze spikes.

He shouted to the kors inside, telling half of them to stay put and the other half to keep walking until they found each other, at least, inside the maze. Then he looked at some of the carvings on the outer wall.

The panels grouped similar things together.

One mural, for instance, pictured a menagerie of beasts: leopards, elephants, herons, alligators, mice, snakes, elks, fish, eagles, and moles, unnaturally entwined. The snarling, trumpeting, wheeling, sniffing, wriggling, clawing figures were carved almost in three dimensions in the black stone.

In another mural were spinning orbs spewing from huge fires amidst wild rippling currents and stars and something like the comet. Strange square symbols were carved next to the objects that were depicted.

Zen could not decipher what the strange markings in the upper right hand corners of the carvings signified. He had seen them in other monuments, and there were a few of the complex markings on his coin. He thought he saw a crude representation of a kor holding a branch in one of the square designs.

The friezes on the outside of the trap were too varied to draw any conclusions from concerning the mysterious halls they enclosed. Zen stepped through the gap in the wall and looked at the panels inside. Rueez stepped in with him.

"Mimu, what are you looking for?" said Rueez.

"I am looking for some clue, some reason for this place," said Zen as he puzzled at a panel to the left of the entrance. On this panel was carved a thing of the head, too, one which was entirely new to Zen and yet entirely clear. "These people could speak without words, Rueez!" he exclaimed.

"What?"

He pointed at the frieze. Carved in the dark rock was a profile of a kor looking at the sun surrounded by rippling rays. His hand held a feather. Carved inside the head of the kor was a little kor who fed a tiny replica of the sun through his lips where it emerged as a stylized furl of wind. Another little kor was carved inside the raised hand that held the feather. This little kor was feeding a miniature sun through his fingertip that emerged on a parchment as a square design with radiating lines.

"I don't get it," Rueez said.

"What do you dain when I say *suuun*, Rueez?"

"Why—the sun, of course."

"But you see, you have changed that," Zen pointed at the sun, "into a bit of wind coming out of your mouth. *Suuun*. These kors changed the sun into this little picture just like we turn it into a little noise. They could speak without talking!"

Rueez looked at the carving. "Ah!"

Zen moved on to the next mural to the right of this one. At the top was a carving of a kor with a feather that connected it to a square hieroglyph:

"Ah, you see, this one means *kor*. It is a silent word, made for the eyes.

Ooooh." Rueez's eyes were wide.

Beneath the first definition was carved a row of many kors side by side, with a feather connecting them to another hieroglyph:

"What is the difference from the first one, Zen?" Rueez was already skeptical of these silent words.

"You see the extra line? That means *many* kors, Rueez."

"Ah."

Zen looked below at the next image.

Pictured on the left was a kor. He was hunched over what were apparently two intricate halves of a puzzle. On one half was a jagged indentation and on the other was a jagged protrusion. The kor's unusually expressive face was screwed up in puzzlement even as Zen's was as he looked at the picture. This scene was connected by a feather to another symbol:

Zen and Rueez puzzled over it for a while and noticed that it had one more line than the symbol for "kor" which was in the central enclosure.

Zen rubbed his beard and furrowed his brow, suddenly widening his eyes and laughing. "What are we doing, Rueez?" he said.

"What?" asked Rueez.

"We're daining! Just like the kor in this picture. This symbol means daining!"

Rueez was silent with awe.

"It's a good thing Azurel taught us that word!" Zen laughed.

"That they could make a few carvings in stone say such hard things," said Rueez, "is truly amazing! And a little scary, almost, eh, Zen?"

"No! Beautiful! A lot of work, maybe…" Zen looked at the corridors around them. "But as long as this wall is teaching us their ancient words we must try to learn what they are saying. It may explain this queer trap. Look at this next part."

The next panel showed the previous image but with the hands of the kor successfully clapping together the halves of the puzzle. A feather connected this to a symbol:

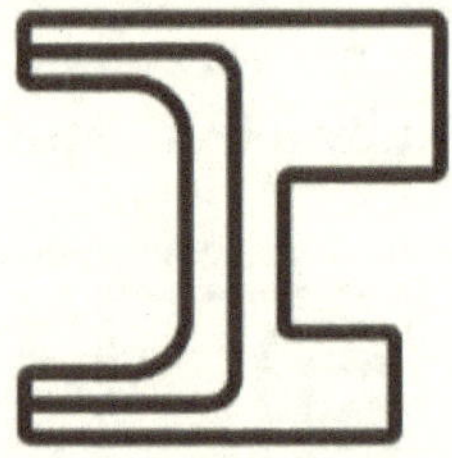

There was a line under this and then a succession of similar symbols. Beside a scene of a hunting kor:

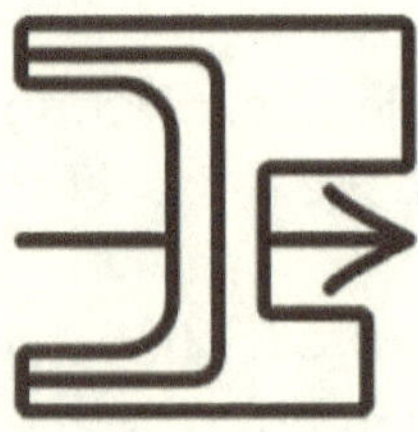

Next to a carving of a kor digging:

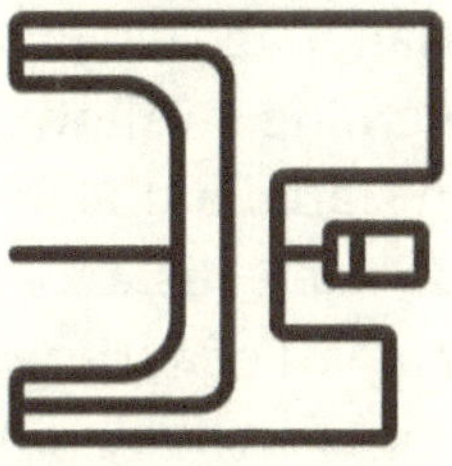

And, beside the picture of a kor building a home:

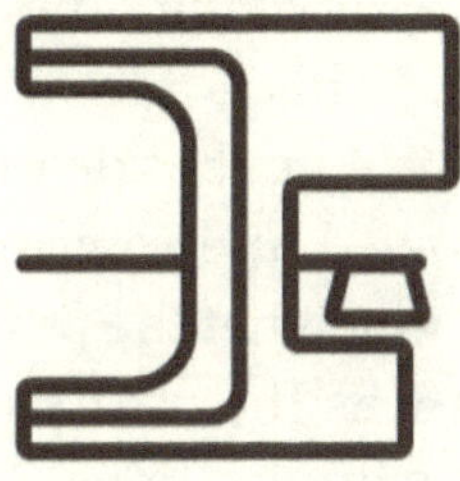

"Yes," murmured Zen. "Yes, yes." He pointed at the symbol for daining. "You see, Rueez, what starts as a thing in the head," he pointed at the inner enclosure with the line through it in the previous pictograph, "becomes something outside, by itself." He pointed at the symbol by the hands successfully solving the puzzle.

"Yes! The first means daining and the next means doing. It's just as Azurel explained it to me," Rueez said. "What we do starts inside our heads, then happens outside. They added these tools to say what they were doing." Rueez pointed at the glyphs below.

"Right!" Zen clapped his hands. "This means hunting, this means digging, this means building."

They moved to the next panel.

This was a deep relief of a strange scene with many glyphs they did not recognize. Kors were pouring some smoking substance into vessels from a great flaming cauldron fanned by kors. This time Zen and Rueez were stumped. If there was any connection between the language lesson and the bizarre activity in this panel, it was something swallowed by time.

Rueez turned as Zen stared at the mural. He glanced along the wall behind them and some distance down the corridor, just around a corner, he saw a part of a frieze depicting more glyphs like the ones before them. "Zen, look down there!"

Zen saw it and immediately walked down the corridor and looked at the mural. It was a list like the list started on the last mural of the lesson, depicting different activities with corresponding symbols. "This is the next part of the lesson," Zen said. "And yet why is it not beside the other panels? This is very strange!" Zen furrowed his brow and worked his jaw.

"Zen, if we didn't know what the first panels say we would never have known this was the next part of the lesson," said Rueez, exasperated at the implications.

Zen turned to Rueez, his blue eyes bright. "Rueez, you have a quick head! That's why the building is so tangled. So that you are forced to learn your way through its halls in order to find your way out! This is a school, Rueez, not a trap. To find your way out, you must graduate!"

"Mimu, do you dain we can learn our way through such a vast place quickly enough to avoid starving?" Rueez's eyes were wary as he cast them from side to side down the four halls of the intersection.

Zen nodded. "We must get food, much of it, and water for the journey. The others will need it when we find them. Then we must go through the school and follow its lessons to the end."

They left to load two travois with provisions, and Zen told the other kors not to follow them and to continue to do their work. If Zen did not return with the others, they should declare the place off limits until they had carefully mapped the tangled course of the great school. He posted two guards by the entrance to see if any kors found their way out. He shouted to the kors inside to search for the tracks of their travois and follow them either out of the maze or to Zen and Rueez.

Then they went to the place in the labyrinth where they had left off and looked down the twisted corridors. A parrot fluttered above and landed on top of the wall, grinning as though it had just seen all the trapped kors from the sky.

"The Truth is in Tai-Raynee!" it screamed, and it flew off again as Zen just missed it with a rock.

From the panels which followed, Rueez and Zen were able to piece together the rudiments of the ancient kor language.

A simple square meant world, and it framed each object.

The square could be modified with a design for a more descriptive backdrop. For instance, a square with an "X" in it:

meant sky. There were others for sea, forest, mountain, shore, and so on.

Only objects were enclosed in boxes, subjects were alone, in the open. The lesson presented a crude sentence after laying down the fundamentals:

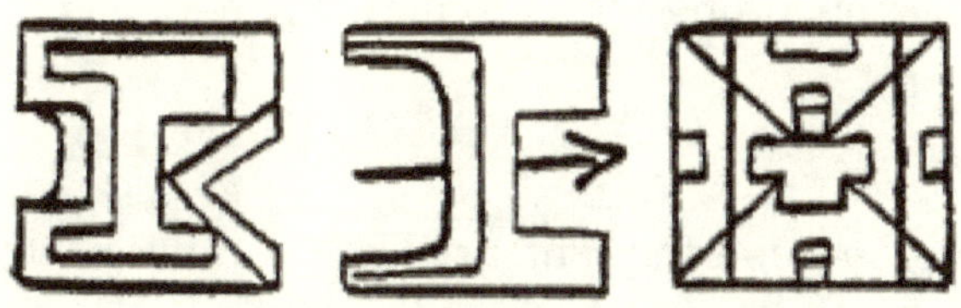

This meant "Kors hunted fowl flying in the forest." After this, the mural assigned other such exercises, defining each carefully with realistically carved images. In order to progress through the corridors, the kors learned a working vocabulary, giving each symbol a spoken word.

The language course took them right on through the night until, bleary at morning, they found little Jeeky weeping in a corner. When Jeek looked up, he screeched and flung himself through the air onto Zen's head. After Zen pried him off he shouted out to Kon that Jeek was unharmed, if a little hungry. "He's eating my ear!" growled Zen.

"Cut it out, Jeeky!"

The mighty Kon was glad but he expressed a loud and lewd consternation in the maze.

"You went in hastily, Kon," Zen chided him. "You cannot force your way out of this place! You must dain your way out. But you do not know the language of these walls, and so now you must wait for me to reach you."

"Yes, Mimu," Kon grumbled.

Zen threw food over the walls so that it might fall in the paths of the hungry kors trapped inside.

"Give little Jeek some food, Rueez. And let us look at the next panel."

Jeek watched silently as Zen and Rueez discussed the language lessons and jumped, seemingly at random, from one wall to another. Jeek knew this was serious, so he didn't fool around. At last they came to a lesson which concluded halfway down the panel ending with a statement:

LEARN TO COUNT

They understood the sentence. The vocabulary lessons had prepared them. They looked around and the symbol for counting was on a panel across the hall, down a corridor. Sighing with relief, they went to this panel and learned numbers. At the end of this lesson was another message:

READ, COUNT, AND LEARN

Feathers connected this statement to the panel beside it, which showed a carving of some white baboons in a tree. But Zen and Rueez could not continue without some rest, so they slept before starting the new course.

Night was falling when they woke. Jeek crawled on Zen's great shoulders to sleep as Zen and Rueez proceeded with tallow torches.

During that night, they found seven kors and in the process learned so many wondrous and difficult things by reading the hieroglyphics and looking at the carved scenes that by dawn they had to rest their heads again.

Zen and Rueez, to the other kors' confusion, sat and discussed what they now knew while they ate the invigorating roots of the white giss. They now understood the principles of the bow and arrow. Also, to Zen's particular joy, they learned the training of beasts in great detail. They had learned the idea of metallurgy, also.

As they progressed through each of these new lessons they were carefully introduced to all relevant visual vocabulary, for which Zen and Rueez had to make up spoken words in order to discuss what they were reading. Many new words were made during these long sessions, a process which left their minds weary and exhilarated, and their ensuing conversation increasingly frustrating to their growing audience, who wondered what they were discussing.

They discovered much about ancient Immurtia in the school now, finding 13 kors sitting in corners with stumped expressions on their faces. Zen took a little time with each to explain what they had learned and where they were now going in the maze. They responded to his news with wide eyes and followed Jeek's example of silence as Zen and Rueez worked their way down the twisting corridors.

Zen and Rueez learned from the walls how to capture cattle, ride red elk, sow grain, make bread, and cut and move great stones. They learned of the wheel and the building of wagons. The lesson seemed to be a basic survey of all the kinds of knowledge in Immurtia, a library of the most important knowledge in the old world. It left them bedazzled and speechless when they came to the original intersection by the exit.

"The end of the maze!" exclaimed Rueez, relieved.

"No," said Zen. "More than 50 kors went into the maze and we have not seen all of them, nor could all of them have crossed behind us and followed our tracks to the exit." The others sighed and ran out into the late sun. Zen and Rueez asked the guards posted outside if any kors had made it out.

"Yes, Kon and two others. Kon bids you luck."

"I'm sure he does," Zen grinned. "How many went into the labyrinth?"

"Fifty or so," said one guard.

"How many exactly," asked Zen of the second guard.

"Fifty-one, Mimu."

"Hmm." Zen rubbed his beard. "This is not the end of the school, Rueez! This is a resting point. See these other murals around the exit?" Zen went inside and pointed at some of the panels in the corridor. "We have not learned about them yet. We must go back in."

"But—" Rueez rolled his eyes and sighed. "Yes, Zen."

And so Zen and Rueez went back in as night fell. Lighting torches and carrying fresh provisions, they found a panel with words they recognized carved into it:

YOU HAVE LEARNED THE FIRST PART OF FOUR
LEARN THE SECOND PART

The second course of the university dealt with domestic knowledge: the milking of animals, the churning of butter, the tending of infants, the symptoms and cures of various illnesses, the preparation of foods. One long gallery exhibited deliciously carved recipes for meals which set Zen's and Rueez's mouths watering. They pushed through some complicated surgical instructions and then through a lesson in tailoring and fashion and grooming and beauty treatments, managing by the end to find ten of the remaining 28 kors who had gotten lost inside the labyrinth.

By late afternoon the next day, Zen and Rueez found themselves at the entrance again. According to the guards, five more kors had wandered out of the school by following the travois tracks. Thirteen were still hopelessly lost inside.

Their minds were reeling and their limbs quaked, but they knew they must go on while they remembered what they did of the language of the ancient kors. Only Zen and Rueez had the knowledge needed to finish the maze and bring those still lost inside to its end. They ate some white giss and refreshed themselves and then reentered the maze as weary dusk fell and the sky glowed a deepening green.

The next course was devoted solely to building, much to Zen's satisfaction. The massive and ingenious industry of the ancient kors was explained in painstaking detail, and Zen made it a priority for his crowded mind to remember these lessons. A long gallery was devoted to the origin of Immurtia, and Zen was reminded of one of the riddles that had not yet been solved.

The kors had discovered two kinds of temples in Immurtia: light and airy temples with tall statues of common things such as fish and wheat and children and fruit and all the good things of the world, and different, enclosed temples with weird symbols and images. It was revealed that the former kind of temple had come first in Immurtia's history. For a long time, these places of world-worship were raised and celebrated. Then, suddenly it seemed, there was an increase in tomb building. Many tombs were raised, grandiose and somber, and more effort was put into them. For their benefit great stones were carved out, transported, and raised, and many kors worked in unison. It was then that the temples had become darker places illustrated with weird images, and symbols of death mingled with strange animals that did not exist.

The third course finally ended with a lesson in Immurtia's irrigation. From the written language with which Zen and Rueez had become familiar, they learned that it was this system that had protected the valley of Immurtia from flooding, landslides, wind, weather, and time itself.

The following day at dawn, Zen and Rueez, accompanied by eight sheepish kioros and kioris, exited the school again, and Zen brooded as the others looked at them in quiet curiosity.

"How many followed the tracks out?" Zen asked one of the guards outside the entrance.

"Four, Mimu," said the young kor.

"Then there is one left," nodded Zen. "Rueez and I will need more white giss to finish the last lesson of the school."

"Yes, Mimu." A boy ran off to the stock place to fetch the roots.

"Zen! Are you sure you can continue?" said Neon, who had been sleeping outside the maze as she waited for him.

Zen smiled. "We must! There is only one more part. It is hard work, but it is worth itself many times over." He kissed her tenderly and she frowned softly, stroking his furrowed brow. "We must go on while it is still fresh in our heads!" he said.

She nodded.

Zen and Rueez took the white giss in their mouths and chewed them, feeling a little false energy entering their chests and fooling their muscles. Then they turned, dragging the travois, to reenter the school when Rueez fell on the grass. The kors gathered around him and tried to rouse him.

"I cannot go on, Mimu!" Rueez's eyes were slitted and tearful. "I want to, but I can't. The muscle in my head is tied in knots."

Zen placed his hand on Rueez's brow. "Rest, then! I could not have made it this far without you. I will finish."

And Zen went back into the school, alone.

The course began with a statement that tested Zen's knowledge of the language to the limit and strained his spinning head:

The two purest nothings
Solid and empty
Had to be
But could not stay apart
And one made the other real
And the other made the one real
And all possibilities
Poured from their union
Ice, fire, and kors.

There was a massive chaos wherein both halves of a mural merged with each other and fragmented into opposing particles on each side of the seam. Then there were explosions and shooting stars like great long-feathered birds.

One ball of stuff emerged. This was, to Zen's perplexity, said to be the world with all its rivers, mountains, lakes and kors.

As he was pondering, Zen found the last sleeping kor and almost passed him by. He revived a weak Anto and gave him some food, waving a hand to persuade him to come along as he went through the last skein of the maze.

The history now entered another phase: the history of kors.

Evidently, kors had lived in Tai-Raynee long before they lived in Immurtia. A great amount of time had passed them there. After many generations, a way of life began to emerge and Zen became increasingly alarmed as that way grew to be very similar to the Way all kors followed in Tai-Raynee.

There were scenes of these early kors hunting and hiding themselves in bramble bushes, exactly like the Way to Hunt, and Zen saw scenes of kors spear-fishing. Then the kors moved away from Tai-Raynee and founded this great city.

Now the history lesson flowered with wondrous images. Kors built and learned and chased their dreams to a point of breathtaking beauty and boldness in Immurtia. Great prosperity followed their efforts, and the topic of the murals shifted from the industriousness of these kors to the excessive affairs of their rulers and the proclamations and projects of their chiefs.

Monuments and tombs were raised for the rulers by the toil of many kors. A fascination with death and with the unknown and with the past infected the best work of kors then. Zen came across a scene of Tai-Raynee exactly like the one in the ziggurat, but here he saw barges on the River Eri with kors and their dead. More and bigger tombs and temples were raised and Zen came upon a lesson on mummification and other solemn rites of death. Finally, at midnight, he came to a carving that took the space of three panels.

The carving was like the one he had seen on the lid of the first tomb they found. He saw it in some of the darker temples, as well. It was the picture of two skeletons bending over a retching kor whose fur was patched and falling. And beneath it was a message:

SICKNESS KILLS MANY KORS

Then there was another great carving, also covering three panels. The first depicted ancient Sor, sitting legless and armless, his slitted eyes at peace. Parrots sat on his shoulders. Several more parrots flew to his right. Covering three more panels, was a carving of Tai-Raynee, the Cinter rising in the center of the plain and a feather connecting the scene to a single glyph that Zen knew meant "everything."

And then the panels were blank.

"The truth is in Tai-Raynee!" cried a parrot as it winged over the maze.

Zen stood before the last mural as its mystery frustrated him. Anto saw the tears of fatigue streaming from the hunter's red eyes and he gripped his shoulder. "Zen, leave this now! Is this not the end?"

"Yes," Zen muttered.

"And so you have done it! Let's go and then you can rest. It is amazing what you have done, Mimu!"

Zen had no words left, and he gripped his face in one hand.

Anto took the travois from Zen's shoulders. "*Mimu,* come!"

Anto helped Zen along as they followed the last chain of blank panels to the entrance of the school, where Neon waited for them.

Zen embraced her and then collapsed into a deep slumber on the grass outside the maze.

Azurel threw blobs of shell-meat at the crabs curling pincers, which fed the blobs through the nostrils of the skulls.

Dozens of skulls squeezed closer around her and she laughed madly as she threw them morsels. By now the crabs had learned to simply follow her around the beach all day for food. She often took them on guided tours, lecturing the attentive faces that never tired of her senseless jabber. In a strange way, they had become her friends. They were docile creatures, and Azurel regretted killing them and sought out other sources of food, instead, simply to spare them.

Her belly was swollen. Her breasts felt tender. She had almost finished carving the kor child in the piece of jade that she had found. She could not choose what sex she would make it. She carried it around her neck on a seaweed cord. She continued to build the foundations of her lonely future, working on her sculpture and trying to ignore what her body was doing.

She looked at the skull-crab she had named Rueez, which was feeding bits of food through its nostrils. Two pains like lightning struck her belly and her head and she fell on the bones, and the skull-crabs inched toward her.

As they scrabbled closer, she finally dained: Kors were more than bones. She rose to her feet.

She had postponed it, but now she must find out. She would not feed Eternity in passive surrender like her staring companions in this grotto.

At dawn, she would enter the cave, again.

In the dark there is nothing but daining, dained Azurel. She could not discern where something ended and nothing began.

The fat shadow-beast charged her in the mud-thick blackness, and Azurel froze in preparation for death as the beast hulked over her. She felt it slobber over her fur and breathe on the back of her head as she crouched beneath it, not believing in it and yet paralyzed by it, until, at last, as though waking, she shouted and lashed out at its blubbery head, startling it backward, its tiny eyes blinking.

Then for a moment she escaped from it, running ahead.

She lit one of her tallow torches and proceeded. But the river of bones beneath her feet grew just as terrifying as the darkness itself and, after miles had passed behind her, the bones flowed like a river around her and somehow she was not moving forward at all.

She heard the beast beyond the reach of her light. It followed her, and mocked her at every step, hurling and crunching its bulk ahead to sometimes watch her from the shadows as she passed.

"Do you know me, kor?" it said.

"No!" she answered.

Could she smell its breath? Or did she dain it, only? There was nothing to compare her dains to, nothing more solid than her fears. "No! How can I know you?" she cried.

"You know me," roared the voice. "You know me, kor! And I will eat you up right now and swallow you!"

"No! You will stand back in the shadow, always."

"I will watch you a little longer, I guess. You and the child that swells inside you."

"Shut up!" Azurel tried to dain of Rueez and her mother and father and sister and brothers and Zen and all the ghosts of daylight that could help her fight this shadow, but she could not conjure them in her head brightly enough, and the beast laughed at her.

"You are burning fires in your brain, kor!"

"I am shouting at me, Horror."

"You know me then!" it shrieked, and its chortling laughter echoed off the high cavern.

Azurel nodded as she stumbled over bones in the total darkness. "You are what kors believe in when they cannot see," she said.

The beast purred. "You do see me, kor."

The cave could be a mile wide, or just over her head. She might have been stumbling perfectly for the past hour through a tunnel that sketched prophetically the outline of her motion through the rock. She had no idea how many stins she had traveled. The world was invisible now, reduced to a few floating skulls in a void that met her falling feet, supporting them into absolute nothingness.

"Why do you go into this evil place, kor?"

She was about to deliver a bitter answer when she suddenly gasped and wept. "I don't know!"

She had little of the crab meat that she had managed to cook at the shore. She had found some flint and roasted two skull-bowls full of meat over driftwood for her journey. But she had lost one skull-full running from the beast the first time. She ate the last gamy remainders now.

She had no way to know it, but more than a week and 15 stins had passed her in the darkness. She drank some false milk from her own breast; an illusory nourishment. Then she got up and walked ahead, lighting a tallow torch every ten minutes to keep her mind alive.

IX

Zen had many dreams that night. He dreamed of flying houses, metal axes, children swinging on gables, waterfalls, making love in stone towers, diving into cool lakes, and spearing ducks in the sky.

He woke, and it seemed in the new daylight that all his dreams were waiting for him, like dains wishing to become deeds.

"Zen! You are awake!" said Neon, and she kissed him, sighing with joy, for she had feared that he might never wake again.

"Yes! Neon, I have been asleep all these years. The kors in Tai-Raynee—they are all asleep, too. They have been sleeping since they left this place. They have been dreaming dark dreams and lost the way to dream in daylight!"

Neon laughed. "Zen, what did you find in the maze?"

Zen sat up on the edge of his bed. His brow wrinkled. "I found—" he frowned, light-headed. "Too many things to say right now. Too many things the maze shouts at me and sings inside my head! All the kors must go through the school, Neon.

Everyone must learn these things so we can rebuild Immurtia and breathe life into the world again."

"Darling Zen, what do you mean?"

"The fire here," Zen whispered, pounding the spiral galaxy on his chest. "The spark in this head." He tapped his head and snapped his fingers. "The light in this eye." He looked at her. "The warmth in this mouth." Zen kissed her. "The dreams in this stone!" He jumped up and hugged the warm fireplace of the feast hall, laughing as though the graven squirrels and snails and foxes tickled his belly.

The next morning, the sky was clear, the sun was gold, and the birds sang in the waving branches. Water coursed down the aqueduct, cutting a brilliant line behind the trees and chattering down the ziggurat. Parrots circled in the sky over Immurtia as Zen looked from beside Neon's fountain at the world with a smile on his face.

At the meeting that morning, he told everyone what he and Rueez had found in the maze. He bade that, one by one, all the kioris and kioros must take the four courses of the school.

Rueez touched his shoulder. "Zen, you have been asleep for ten days!"

Zen looked at Neon, who laughed apologetically. "I'm sorry I did not tell you."

"Well! That's why I feel dizzy," Zen said, and some little children giggled.

"I taught old Char the first course," said Rueez, "and he has proceeded through all four courses already. Now he is guiding others. He has already shown the crafters how to dain and read and count, so they have all gone through the first three courses in groups. Some of the hunters and hearthkeepers and crafters and tanners have gone through, too. Even Kon went through the first course!"

"Kon?" Zen exclaimed.

"We know how to dain already, Rueez, or else we wouldn't have gotten two steps through that place," Kon said, nodding at the crafters.

Zen turned to Neon, who shrugged before he turned back to Rueez. "Hmm. Quick kors! Very quick! Well, this is marvelous! Our next step is to see what we can do with what we know. I would like, for instance, to train some apes, and maybe some cats. That would save time from hunting to work on other things in Immurtia."

"Yes," Char said. "That is a good dain. We can train some red elks for riding and hauling, like the lessons in the maze."

"Have the crafters been able to build those spear-throwers?" Zen asked.

Kem came forward. "Yes, Mimu. We are still perfecting them."

"Good. We can knock ducks down from the sky with those. And cats will retrieve them for us! What about the stones they melted for axe heads and so forth?"

"It is a process we have not learned well enough. But we are trying."

"Ah well, in time! How are the stocks of food?"

"We could use a little more," said Kon, who as a rule always believed in having a little more.

"Very well. Kon, take your troop hunting today with any others who choose to. I will take my troop to capture some apes, if we can."

Happily, the hunters, tanners, hearthkeepers, and crafters bid each other good travels before splitting up and heading out in different directions from the ziggurat.

Zen remembered vividly the lesson on the capture and taming of white baboons. He had dreamed it in his long sleep, and it seemed like a memory already.

The process was very different from the capture and taming of forest cats. Force was needed with the ferocious cats; they had to be captured, wrestled and subdued since superior strength alone impressed them. Whereas cats must be placed within a hierarchy, there was a different method for apes. First, they must be captured and distributed among households, where they would be fed and treated well for a few weeks before they would develop trust and friendship with kors. After a while, their confinement should be slackened and, ultimately, they must be allowed to socialize freely with their own kind at all functions where kors socialized. Only then would apes hunt with kors and guard their homes.

In the forest that day, Zen and his troop had no luck finding any baboons. But they did bag a few deer, and after they had searched for many hours, they found a litter of forest cat cubs in an unguarded burrow. The snarling kittens were striped purple-and-white. Zen noted that they were past weaning, so he promptly had his troop take them. When they turned to go, both parents returned.

These were impressive purple tigers, who were quite prepared to fight. Zen, Tuton, and Rueez dropped their travois, preparing to strike at them. Then Zen remembered that no weapons could be used in capturing them. The punishing strength of a single kor was required in order to discourage the cats from fighting kors. This, Zen realized suddenly, was no easy assignment!

"If only Win were here," he muttered. "Tuton! You will have to wrestle the tigress, on the left. You may not use your weapons unless you must kill it. Remember, we are trying to capture these animals and not destroy them."

"Why?" asked Tuton.

"Now, Tuton," Zen said.

"Zen, I will go!" Rueez said.

"No, Rueez," Zen said. "After all, you are not powerful enough to wrestle a tiger, and I am not sure that I am, either. Tuton, can you?"

"I will try, Mimu," said Tuton, looking at the cats, grimly.

"Very well then. Go!"

They dove on the surprised tigers, who snarled and whined below them as the kors wasted no time. As soon as Zen landed on the back of the fleeing male tiger, he wove his arms under the cat's forearms and over the back of its neck, interlocking his fingers. He then wrapped his legs around its hind legs and rolled over so that the beast was on top of him, belly-up. The cat was strong, but Zen was stronger. It tried to convulse free and very nearly did. But Zen squeezed the cat to within a breath of death.

Tuton had a more difficult time. The female purple tiger got away from him the first time and lunged, knocking him over and taking a nip out of his chest. It wasn't too serious, and in fact it angered Tuton so as to give him a blinding burst of strength. He nearly finished the great cat with a mighty headlock before following Zen's example.

"We must wait, Tuton," said Zen, who laid next to him under the heavy cat.

"What?" said Tuton.

"We must show the cats our strength," Zen said. "They will become gentle soon, and then, according to the school, they will obey us! But only when they become gentle. Hold on until then, Tuton."

Tuton whimpered.

"Soon" was a word that was not taught in the school. The cats tried to thrash free for a long time.

Zen stubbornly had them wait a full three hours, despite the exasperation of Tuton and the others. "Immurtia was not built in a day," he told them over the roar of the tigers. Finally, Zen had the others leave some meat from the deer for them and go back to the city.

Another three hours passed.

The sky was cooling and if anyone was becoming docile it was Zen and Tuton.

"Zen, I'm bleeding and tired and I'm holding a tiger," Tuton told him.

"I'm dizzy, and I haven't been awake for ten days. And I'm holding a tiger," Zen replied, and they both laughed as the shadows lengthened.

Then the cats started purring.

"Pet her chest, Tuton!" Zen whispered.

"What?" said Tuton.

"*Shhh!* We must show them we do not intend to harm them, or they, like any beast, will not be content."

This made sense to Tuton, given the circumstances, and he carefully tweaked the back of the cat's ear, reluctant to break his grip. The strange purring sound grew.

Ever so slowly, they relaxed their grips on the cats, a change which the animals did not seem to notice. As night settled, Zen got up and set the male tiger on its feet. Its tail switched as it looked sideways at Zen, making queer little noises, its whiskers bristling. It nudged his leg with its ribs. Zen raised his brows at Tuton.

Tuton did the same with his tiger, and then Zen led both cats to the deer meat. He picked up a haunch of the venison, nodding at Tuton to do the same, and they handed the offerings to the cats, who took them with quiet, amazed gratitude.

Then Zen and Tuton petted the tigers and roughhoused with them a bit, making sure to exhibit an upper hand in the tumbles and knowing well the pressure points on all beasts that could immobilize or kill them with their practiced hands. They then tied thick leather straps on either side of the tigers' forelegs and attached strong leads to these. They petted them again, confidently and briskly, fanning their front paws, stretching the claws, and stroking their necks as the school had instructed.

Shouldering their travois, they led their bewitched cats into Immurtia.

The stars were bright gold. The palm trees by the long lake glistened as they swayed to the rhythm of the frisky wind. The lavender planets bobbed on the surface of the lake. Tuton and Zen led the 300-pound cats toward the cheerful, luminous waterfall on the ziggurat.

Tallow torches winked on the courtyard above and in the eleven towers that still rose around hit; it was the Fifth Night and the kors were celebrating their miraculous new knowledge.

As they approached the sibilant waterfall, Zen's tiger seemed to break out of its spell. It turned on its leash and leaped at Zen. Zen roared terrifically, and with his fist, he smote the cat, landing a blow that would have cracked a kor's skull.

The cat fell on its side and rolled, stunned gravely but unharmed. It sat low, blinking dramatically. It was then that it remembered the strength of the kors as it lay resigned on the grass, licking its paw, its big ferocious face pouting as it rubbed its head. Zen threw it a piece of meat, and after it gulped down the tidbit, Zen petted it again, and led it along firmly, patting its neck every so often. Tuton followed Zen's example of firm encouragement with his cat, which was smaller and more amenable.

They climbed the three stories in the three towers and walked down the causeway to join the celebration with the purple tigers.

The other kors were awed by the beautiful beasts the hunters had bewildered, and they gathered around as the cats nudged Zen's and Tuton's knees. Then, Zen and Tuton led them to some benches around one of the fires far enough away that the cats were not alarmed. There, they gave the cats flanks of roasted antelope, and the cats purred and slavered over the food until they were sated. Tuton and Zen took their dinner then, and they laughed as they toasted each other with berry wine.

"You would have made your father proud today, Tuton, as you've made me proud!" Zen said.

Tuton shook his head.

Zen told the group of hunters gathered around the fire how they managed to tame the ferocious beasts. "And we got six cubs which will be easy to tame and make at home with us."

"Yes, they're beautiful!" said Sannava, who leaned on Anto's arm. "I saw them over there at the corner of the courtyard!"

"Well, by all means, go over there, Anto, and make sure they do not wander into the sight of these two here," said Zen. "In fact, get some boys and girls to take them downstairs into one of the rooms below and look after them there. Give each a gourd of elk milk to keep them quiet. They shouldn't see their parents for a year, at least."

Anto's eyes popped and he promptly left.

"We can tame the white baboons and the red elk, too," Zen continued. "The red elk are easiest. We just have to mount them and ride them, and soon they will cease to fight and jump and they will be tame. And we can harvest their milk. Oh, by the way." Zen searched the glowing faces quickly. "Kem! You are one of the crafters. Did you see the strange leather gear used to harness the red elk? We shall need such gear. Also, could you make strong harnesses for these tigers tomorrow?"

"Yes, Mimu, we will! Very strong ones, you can be sure. We also have a number of spear-flingers ready tomorrow for you to see."

"Splendid. Tuton, you should take your tiger to your home and remember the proper way to treat it."

Tuton nodded, wincing as his wife, Seenay, washed the bloody gash on his chest. She applied an unguent of herbs and oils Char had made from lessons in the school.

"We must keep them captive for a time before they learn to stay with us." Zen scratched the ear of the big male, who lay content at his feet. "They respect us kors," grinned Zen, his teeth gleaming in the firelight. "We are strong, and good, also."

They celebrated long that Fifth Night in the great city under the stars, and even the cats got drunk as they slurped unguarded cups. At midnight, a lone parrot cried high and melancholy over the ziggurat: "The Truth is in Tai-Raynee!" And Zen and the others laughed and dained no—the Truth was in Immurtia.

"We must really teach those old birds something new," said Char, and Neon nodded, smiling against Zen's shoulder.

X

The Korensis had been busy in Tai-Raynee. They worked night and day to enforce the new law Tor decreed: The new would be permitted only when it replaced the old.

The Korensis worked night and day to dismantle all new buildings and burn the homes of the families that had left with Zen. Yet the grief shadowing Tai-Raynee came of a different meaning in Tor's law: Children would be permitted only if they were replacing the old. The Korensis had been employed in the public killing of newborns, or of grandparents who could not bear to see their grandchildren die. The blood of kors was staining the Korensis' hands and working a change upon their hearts. The cruelest among them became the most powerful.

The feast of the Fifth Day was banned, and a strange poverty resulted. There was no more weekly indulgence, but there were suddenly shortages of all kinds.

The laughter and singing were quieted. Only wails of mourning and the humble groans of the devout echoed unchallenged in the still of dawn.

The sors presided over all, and over them holy Tor, in place of Ez. Tor alone among the sors sat on top of his stone instead of before it, armless, legless and attended by three servants.

"Go, and take apart that building yonder," he said now, and the Korensis, who stood in rows at the ready behind Tor, sent out a group to carry out his word.

He spoke little, but people feared the words he spoke. No one dared lift a hand against him. Even white On acquiesced to his whispered insights, and his face seemed tired and fearful before the prophet.

In order to enforce the law of Tor, many of the young kors in Tai-Raynee were drafted into the Korensis, castrated by the crafters and sworn to the oath of service. The example of Tor rendered opposition impossible. The kioris and kioros of Tai-Raynee became the arms, legs, and ears of holy Tor, reporting to him the sins of those who opposed him and carrying out his executions. The days passed without deviation, without remark.

And as Tor foretold, the great ghost in the sky had gone away on the night he became a sor.

Turi saw a great white mountain too bright to look at. Nevertheless, he was drawn to it, and at last his eyes discerned shapes and outlines as the light turned red and dimmed. Then he saw, all heaped pitilessly on a pile rising higher and higher into the sky until it resembled a crimson Cinter, a giant melting mound of kor legs and arms and heads.

He woke up, gasping and cold. As he stared at the roof of his Artist's home in the gray morning, he knew he could no longer be an Artist. He could no longer create. There was no art left inside him.

And so, trembling, he went to his brother, who was no longer his brother, but holy Tor, a power without form, a will without name, a person without past, a past without person.

Tor looked down from the block of stone. "What, Artist?"

"Holy Tor, I can make no more art. I had an evil dream, and can no longer make art. There is nothing inside me to make!"

Tor turned his head and looked into his eyes. "Nor can there ever be. That is not the purpose of Art. What was your dream, Artist?"

"I dreamed of a great hill of flesh, of kioro and kiori and child cut and broken and piled high! It was terrible to dream such a dream..."

"If it was terrible, you must create it."

Turi looked upon his mutilated brother, his last work of art. "No..."

"This," said Tor, "is the work of Art you must create to show all there is nothing inside you that you would invest in this false world, no feelings for the Immurtai, no concern for your life or for the life of any kor. You must build your dream—the Amoli has inspired you. This is how you will teach kors the humbling and ultimate Truth. The forever Truth before which all else is false."

Turi stammered. "But—of stone. I will carve it in stone, of course."

Tor shook his head slowly. "Of flesh. As you dreamed it."

"No! Brother—holy Tor—stone does not decay like the lie of the flesh. Stone lasts forever, as befits the *Demurtai*, stone does not unravel and crumble away as does the flesh!"

"Stone lasts no longer than flesh, to the Amoli," Tor said, as he looked at the sky. "Make it of flesh. When we do such as this, Artist, we deny the *Demurtai* a place here, and the here a place in the *Demurtai*. Nothing could please the Amoli more. It is the only Truth. Their union is false and blasphemous. The greatest danger is that these two things, the Immurtai and *Demurtai,* will mingle inside kors. When this happens, disasters like the one in the sky may bring an end to the *Koroshi* itself, as though it were any other thing. Don't you see?"

"But of stone!" Turi protested.

"Of flesh. Take as many Korensis as you may require to collect the kors that are needed."

"You're starving, kor."

Azurel had lost her flint and her tallow torch had burned out. "Why do you seem so real?" she whispered.

"Because you know nothing of death, of darkness, of Eternity," whispered the beast.

Azurel's mind was numb to the thing's riddles. She touched her temple and winced. "This tunnel is never-ending."

"Watch your step, kor."

Azurel had climbed a seemingly endless incline of skulls until her head struck stone. She had touched the ceiling! Was this the end of the cave? She dug through the skulls, casting them down the hillside behind her with one hand as she held her bulging stomach with the other. She felt the life inside, waking even as she approached death. She had no more food. The world was all blackness. The beast climbed up the slope of bones behind her.

"Kor, I am so very hungry. Kor, I will eat you right up."

The beast vanished, banished by the tiny glint of real light she saw over the bones.

The next day, the valley almost hummed with activity. Even little children pulled weeds from between stones and berries from the swaying trees.

Zen and Tuton brought the purple tigers with them on the hunt. Afterward, they worked with the beautiful beasts on the grass by the tannery to train them to obey. Kors practiced shooting arrows from bows. There were groups in the maze, and other kors were clearing the cobbled roads in the forest and building homes.

Kon's hunting troop was gone longest that day, and when they returned, he was riding a very tired-looking red elk. Five of the other kors in his troop also rode elks, and each one of these led three more on tethers.

Everyone applauded their feat, and at dusk, as the hearthkeepers set about preparing meals in the many homes throughout the valley, the young and spirited hunter kioros and kioris rode the remaining untamed red elks to try and break them in. There was much laughter as kors were thrown for loops. Tuton tried and was tossed into the lake. His tiger, whom he had named Leza, ran and pounced on him in the water to further confuse him. But the cat was only bedeviling him, and its coarse tongue almost tore his nose off as poor Tuton tried to scramble away and climb out of the water. Then, from the shore, he dove and tackled the mischievous cat, which purred loudly as they wrestled. Both kor and tiger were deadly beasts and seemed to know now that death would be the sad alternative to friendship.

Before dark, the hunters gathered, cut trees, and made a high stable for the elks. Then they went off to dinner.

Zen invited all his good friends to eat with him in the feast hall that night. Clean and beaming, his guests arrived. Kon came with his wife, Buri, and his children, and Tuton with Seenay, and Rueez, and Char. Then came Anto with Sannava, who had come in a strange and enticing garment of leather, and Sara. Then came Jak and his family, and some other great hunters of old Tai-Raynee and their families soon arrived. Zen and his sons had made fine furniture; the saws enabled them to make the long table and benches flat-surfaced, but they heard another tool the crafters had made that could cut wood even more easily. Torches lit the long hall, and logs burned in the carved fireplace. The stone floor was smooth and clean thanks to Neon, and a well-fed and snoozing purple tiger lay by the fire in the sturdy leash the crafters had made.

After the steaming food was served, Zen quieted the guests and proposed a toast to them.

"To Win!" he said, and everyone drank deep.

They ate the stewed giss and venison and roasted rabbit and fowl, and they drank the berry wine which was once again in store. And they danced and sang before the fire as Zen and the great hunters told tales and boasted.

Little Jeeky's sister was even littler. Her eyes were larger than his, and bright green in a sunlit brown face. Flowerina presented Zen with a green and red flower. "Bumble-mumble, Mimu," she confided, pouting into his ear after pulling his beard.

"Umble-uh?" Zen grunted.

"Hee-mumbled me, Mimu," she sighed.

"Mumblety-who?" whispered Zen, concerned.

"Bee mumbled me, bumble-bee-boo!" she giggled, slapping his nose with her tiny hand.

"Be-humbled be Mimu, too!" laughed Zen, shrugging sadly at the little girl.

"Bumble bee stung me, Mimu!" she scolded, holding up her swollen finger.

The table roared with pent-up laughter.

"She stung her finger picking you a flower, Zen!" said Kon. "You should be honored!"

"Well, I am!" Zen laughed, his chest rocking. "Humbled me, jumbled me, and bumbled be Mimu!" He lifted little Flowerina onto his arm and she clapped her hands, looking at everyone and laughing.

"How do you like this, Zen?" said Sannava, posing in a garment of leather. Anto was embarrassed at her side, for the garment was somehow very exciting to look at.

"It is marvelous," Zen grinned. "It makes a red-blooded kor want to rip if right off, eh Hunters?" he laughed, and Jak and Kon laughed, too, in appreciation.

Sannava spun on a toe, smiling. "Another thing we kioris learned from the maze." Sannava glanced at Anto mischievously as she posed, and he smiled back raising one brow.

"Soon, all the kioris will dress like this," old Char predicted, nodding his silver head. "That will be nice."

"We'll decorate the kioros, too! There are some very interesting designs in the maze," said Sannava.

"Oh," said Zen, but he didn't finish. He wished the rest of Tai-Raynee could see all the things they were discovering.

"Zen," Char said. "Remember we dained Sor must have taught the parrots their words?"

Zen nodded.

"I found something yesterday. Remember the legend of the white kor who lived in the forest long ago?"

"What white kor, old Char?" shouted Jeeky.

"*Shhh*, now, I'm talking to Zen," grouched Char.

"But what white kor, tell me the story!"

With that, Old Granny Kori awakened. She was over 100 years old and Jeeky's great-grandmother, and her knobby face was nearly bald of her wispy white fur. She had been sitting up and sleeping in her chair by the fire, but now one of her amber eyes popped open at little Jeeky and she grinned a scary old smile.

"Will you tell Jeeky the story of the white kor, granny Kori, so Zen and I can talk?" Char winked.

Jeeky looked at his great-grandmother in delicious fear.

"Well," her voice scratched like a lizard's claw, "he's old enough now, I guess!"

Char grinned. "And don't hold back! All the terrible details," he nodded.

"Why? Is it that scary?" worried Jeeky.

"Maybe he's too young," Granny Kori frowned.

"No, no! I want to hear it!"

The other children clamored to hear, too, so Granny Kori led them outside with a tallow torch to tell the children the story by the flickering glow of the candle, leaving the adults at least a full hour of peace.

"Good work, Char," nodded Kon.

"What a dear is Granny Kori! Now, Zen, I found something yesterday. I found the bones of a kor in a room inside the ziggurat by the maze. The room was stocked with skins and food, very old, but not as old as Immurtia. And the skeleton was missing the right thumb and had white fur."

"So?" shrugged Kon.

"So maybe the legend of the white kor was about a sor?" asked Rueez.

"Maybe. Their fur is turned white by the black giss. A fallen sor who left Tai-Raynee centuries ago and then found this city."

"That would make sense," said Zen.

"And if that's so, it explains some of the words the parrots say. I think they learned them from this sor, and not the original Sor. You notice how they say 'the Secret of Sor' and 'Tai-Raynee, old parrot, you've only to look'?"

Others in the room laughed as Char parroted the parrots.

"Well, Zen, why would Sor talk about 'the Secret of Sor'? Would he shout about a secret he was keeping by getting these birds to shout about it? It could have been this old sor, who left Tai-Raynee and found this place, who taught the parrots these mocking words."

"So," said Zen. "He found Immurtia and discovered the Secret of Sor that was hidden from Tai-Raynee for so long."

"Unless the Secret of Sor is hidden in Tai-Raynee." Char shrugged.

"That is a story to dain on, Char," said Zen. "I should like to see that skeleton. But we will teach the parrots new words, now, eh?"

The kors laughed.

"There is a mystery in it, Zen," said Char. "Some hidden thing pulls and changes the words the parrots speak. What truth is in Tai-Raynee? Why was there truth in Tai-Raynee? What was in Tai-Raynee that made the kors leave here? It is too dark now, too distant, and too many pieces are missing." Char sighed, taking some wine. "You're right, Zen. We should teach the birds new things to say now," he toasted.

Zen looked into the fire, around which danced laughing children. Whatever grim truth might be in Tai-Raynee he did not care to know.

Azurel opened the breach, digging away the bones, and pulled herself through. She slid all the way down the slope on the far side.

At the bottom of a wide pit, she climbed knee-deep in bones that cut her legs up the far rise. She felt patches of fur and the bones of hands and limbs and ribs as she rose higher on the slope.

She smelled a terrible, cold stench of fresh death around her and she reached out to the glimmer of light that had drawn her and touched a child's skull at the top of the mound.

Patches of fur grimaced on the charred bone of the face. For a moment she imagined bright obsidian eyes looking gleefully at her from the empty sockets. One tooth was missing, the left front tooth.

Her artist's eye knew with certainty that it was the skull of little Erg.

She swooned and staggered forward over the hill of bones, sliding down its far side until the bones receded before a smooth floor layered deep with fine ash.

She saw a leaping antelope painted on the wall in the weird, bloody glow.

Another image of an antelope was painted beside it, and other images all around. She could see kors and geese and fish in a river and a dragonfly, and there were glowing rocks in the ceiling above.

To her left there was a tall mantle of stone. In a crack above it sat a large-jawed skull with wide black eyes, illuminated by red tallow torches placed around it in a circle. Crouching before it were the silhouettes of 21 sors.

Under the skull sat an armless and legless kor, his fur snow-white, his black eyelids closed.

Azurel was weak and weary and dizzy with hunger, but anger warmed her blood now as the halves of the puzzle came together: the limbs on the shore and the limbless kor; the tunnel of bones and the cave of the sors; the infinite shadow and the bones of little Erg.

Hugging the wall, she passed the sors and went out of the cave into the midnight wind over sleeping Tai-Raynee.

She walked from the Cinter, laughing tears as she traveled familiar roads.

She stopped at some stock houses and ate food until she could not chew and drank fresh water until it spilled down her jaw. She took two skins of water, dried meat, and white and brown giss in a strap-basket.

Then she went back to the Cinter, which hung like a monster on the fading night sky. The stars were good and golden tonight and she looked hard at the glorious world. Dawn would soon arrive. She lingered outside the cave, wanting to see the sun and the colors it would bring.

In the gray shades before morning, she could see the blackened earth left by fires throughout the Hunters' province. She could feel the pain Tai-Raynee had suffered.

Some Korensis with spears approached the cave from below. They saw her. Azurel smiled. She did not care even as they shouted and ran. No kors in Tai-Raynee except the sors could follow Azurel where she was going.

The Korensis would be stopped by the sors, and the sors would not be able to catch her. She could see better in the dark than they could now.

Turi was leaving the cave when he saw Azurel's pregnant silhouette at the entrance. He doubted his eyes until she neared and he was sure.

She made a lewd gesture at the Korensis and, much to their dismay, bolted past Turi, without seeing him. He turned in awe and watched her run on fleet and quiet feet. The Korensis followed, but Azurel was down amidst the bones before the Korensis reached the sors, and Turi said nothing to them.

He turned and left, a dangerous will stirring his frozen heart.

She heard voices behind her, and Azurel smiled as they stayed behind, fading.

She came to the wide pit into which she had fallen earlier. Defying her rage, her knees gave way, worn beyond their limit and she slid through the rattling bones till there was no light behind her at all. But the beast was not there, this time.

She dug a hollow in the bones and sat down to drink another long draught of clean water. The baby inside her stirred with new vigor.

She held her statues, which had saved her sanity. She felt their unique shapes in the shapeless sameness of the dark.

She wiped her chin, resolved in one thing. She would slash the sors' throats. She would throw their bones into the forever that they worshipped and set kors free to live for life, however brief, instead.

She heard bones cracking in the distance and lay still.

The sounds grew near and stopped. A spark scratched the air as a tallow torch lit the face of Turi, the Artist.

Azurel seized a bone in a fist as Turi spoke.

"Azurel, you are here! I know you are! Let me help you," he whispered.

She lowered the bone and watched Turi silently.

"Azurel, oh, I am lost! Help me! I will help you!" Turi fell to his knees and he sobbed in his hands. He looked like his statue to her.

"Come here, then," said Azurel.

Turi looked up, smiling, his eyes shining in the glow. "You are here!" he hissed. "It is you? Not a dream?"

"Come here, Turi. If you are lying to me, I will kill you."

"I would rather die than lie to you! I would rather die than go on lying to myself, and all the world." Turi approached and gave her a strap-basket full of food and weapons.

"What of my family?" Azurel asked. "It was you who caused their fate. Tell me how they are now. I saw their lands, scorched and razed."

Turi fell to his knees again. "They and many hunters left Tai-Raynee. They are the lucky ones."

Turi told her what had come to pass in Tai-Raynee while she was away.

Azurel looked into his eyes and finally nodded. "What should be done? You know best what we can do."

"I do, it is true. I have sinned greatly, Azurel. Yet it has given me a power others do not have."

"Then stand up and don't kneel for any more of their Eternity, Turi. Stand up to their lies however big they seem!"

Turi stood. "I will! As soon as I can, I will bring more food and other things that you will need. You are with child…" Turi laid a gentle hand on her belly. She glared at him, and he took his hand away. "I will help you bring the child, when the time comes. And after, I will come for you, Azurel, and we will slip into the cave and slit the sors' throats, together."

"What time will that be, Turi?"

"I do not know. But I will know when it comes."

And Turi crawled away, as quiet as a spider.

Turi obtained as many bodies of elderly kors as he could from the Korensis for the work of art Tor had ordered him to create. He found the Korensis who were about to burn their bodies and wash their bones for delivery to the sors and diverted them to his purpose instead.

On the Second Day, Tor complained to Turi that there were too many gray-haired bodies in the mound he was raising. So Turi tried dyeing some of the parts with paints and oils and using the fur of animals.

The work destroyed his heart, as Tor predicted. He labored without sleep to disguise the body parts of animals and elderly kors who committed suicide so that their grandchildren might live to look like the fresh sacrifices the sors seemed to expect when they came by to inspect his progress. He could not bear that another kor would lose his life for his art.

Yet on the Third Day, Tor complained that there were no children or young kioris on the mound he was creating.

And so on the Fourth Day Turi was forced to choose among the living. He chose one child, and one kiori. And after he was finished that day, he knew his life was worth nothing, worse than nothing.

He told Tor and Tor nodded. "I name you the High Artist of the *Koroshi,*" Tor said. "Only now have you graduated."

And when Turi left, his eyes broke away from the sunlit world, forever.

Days passed before Turi crept back into the forbidden place. He crawled over the bones until he reached the place where Azurel was. Only there did he hazard to make a noise or light a flame.

Azurel saw the light and it woke her staring eyes. "Turi?" she asked.

"It's me."

"You brought tallow torches? Thank you!"

Turi came close, and in the candlelight Azurel saw his ugly face, made handsome, now, with a desperate concern. "Your child is coming close," he said.

"You came in time. My child comes now."

Tears rolled down his face. "May I help?"

"I hope you will."

Turi sighed. He lit more torches, setting them in river shells on the bones around Azurel. With shaking hands he unrolled two sloth furs and laid one out for her to lie on. Then he laid out bags of water and oil. "Drink some pink wine." He held a skin to her lips and she drank.

He braced her knees and held her hands as the birth waves heaved through her body. He saw the baby's furry face emerge, and with his washed and oiled hands, he helped it enter the world.

The baby gasped and cried loud into the darkness. It opened blue eyes and looked at Turi.

"Beautiful!" he whispered, as Azurel's nails cut into his arms. "Push!"

She drew the strength of her life into a single cry as she pushed.

Turi pulled, easing the effort, and in the next moment he held the infant, covered with the blood of birth, in his arms and he wept silently over it.

He cut the mother-cord with the same blade he used to cut his brother's arms—the same tool Azurel had given to him. And then he poured warm water from a flask over the infant and Azurel.

"This is the hunter Rueez's daughter," Turi smiled. He no longer hated Rueez. He loved him for giving him this moment.

Azurel laughed in agony's aftermath. "Yes!"

"I see his nose! Look how serious and calm she is, Azurel!" He laid the baby on her breast and poured warm water gently over them both and over her belly and legs. Then he wrapped the mother cord and placenta in an orange orchid to plant beside the seed of an iris tree, as was the Hunter tradition.

Turi made a bed beside her out of the other sloth fur and helped her onto it. He drew a thin blanket of soft doeskin over her and gave her a pillow of blue weasel fur stuffed with black goose down. After giving her a last drought of purple tiger's blood and rose wine, he left her sleeping with the child suckling her. He looked at them both before he blew out all the torches, except for one that would burn until she woke.

The sun sank slowly in purple and green, and once again the images in the cave faded.

Tor looked with white eyes into the lost eyes of Sor, searching that precious shadow.

The pungent smoke of green manthril flowers rose in thin lines.

The sors listened to the gentle cry of agony far away, and though they heard it they did not mark it with a word. More than one believed they heard the sound of a kiori who lay dying.

Never had they heard a restless ghost in the great tunnel of past and future which they guarded from the present. It frightened even white On to hear the throes of anguish stirring its perfect silence.

When the cries ended, instead of the peace they expected death to bring, they heard the tiny cries of a child waking inside the infinite silence, haunting them.

Then there was silence until the dawn.

When they left the cave that morning, carrying holy Tor, they found the phantom in the sky had returned.

It shone in the daytime, flying right at Tai-Raynee like a great bird from the south, and even the sors were staggered in horror by the sight.

Immurtia churned with activity over the next week. Zen and his troop harvested two dozen antelope in a bola-field, so they were free to pursue a few other things they had longed to do for a while.

Zen and Tuton used their time to continue training their tigers to attack and to retrieve animals, and after a few more preliminary confrontations, and a few nice scars, the cats respected and trusted them enough to surrender game to them. Their relationship with Zen and Tuton became steadfast, and the cats seemed to become good-natured in their new surroundings. Zen named his tiger Tuno.

Meanwhile, the kors perfected their skills in archery and elk-riding. They built wagons on wheels and tried new recipes, and some wore beautiful garments they had made, and they continued to improve their homes and have parties where they showed off their progress.

In the following week, Zen managed to capture, through a sort of bribe, six white baboons. They were intelligent creatures, who smiled and nodded at the kors when they set out meat for them. They had large fangs but were surprisingly gentle and respectful. "Kor, yes, kor," they nodded, and it was evident to the shocked hunters that the apes had preserved and passed down, as had the parrots, a few crude words given them by the ancient Immurtians.

Still, they had to capture the apes to persuade them to live in the city. They were frightened on the journey, apparently taking themselves for kor food, but when they found, after a few days in kor households, that they were welcome and wanted there, they relaxed, and although they would have bolted without leashes, they were obedient. Very soon, however, they became as members of the kors' families, and they were given names and made accustomed to frequent baths.

Neon named her family's baboon Willy. Tuno and Willy had a jealous but civil relationship, both being haughty beasts.

Some of the hearthkeepers found, to their reassurance, that the baboons were excellent baby-sitters, able to climb the trees as agilely as the pranksome children in order to police their mischief. They soon established an amusing upper hand with the mischievous little kor children in the trees above.

On the Fifth Day, the comet reappeared in the sky.

Like a splendid golden eagle burning in the green day instead of the night, it frightened the kors that morning, so Zen gathered all the kors together on the ziggurat of flowing water to speak to them.

Their new way of life in Immurtia was only increasing his desire to contact Tai-Raynee to show them what they had discovered. He took the comet as the sign to go.

Zen spoke to them: "Hunters! Here we have all been free to make our lives as good as our hearts would have and the world will allow."

The Hunters hailed Zen.

"It is time we show the people of Tai-Raynee this better way," he said. "It is time we show them they need not huddle around the Cinter and should not be afraid to be kors in this good world."

"No, Zen!" said Char gravely. "The sors will not listen to this. This place is named Immurtia! Remember?"

Zen frowned. "Bah! How can they deny it when they see? We will show all of Tai-Raynee the truth even if the sors look the other way. And then it won't matter. If we ride in on red elks with our beetleback axes and spears and our tigers and baboons and arrow-flingers, surely none but the blind would not cheer and gather round to see what we have found! And when we tell them of this place, they will know there is a better way. I will go alone to tell them if no one joins me. Tomorrow!" Zen pounded the spiral galaxy on his chest.

"No, Zen!" Char said.

"I will go, as well, Mimu," said Rueez. "I feel like I do not know what has become of me, not knowing what's become of Azurel."

"I'll go," said Tuton.

"And me," said Kon.

"And me," said Jak.

"And so will I, if I must," Char said sadly. "But I hope you are right, Zen.

How can I not be?" Zen smiled, and he waved his hand across the city.

XI

The next day, Zen, Rueez, Jak, gray Char, Tuton, Kon and some of their sons said goodbye to their wives and children.

They found themselves glancing sadly at the valley around them as they rode their tall elks up the northern ridge. Neon's violet eyes were sad when they last touched Zen's, and he left with a faint frown on his face that lingered for many stins.

The tigers, Leza and Tuno, and six snow-white baboons padded along beside them on tethers. They traveled quickly through the forest that day and camped that night by the glistening lake, allowing the elks to graze on tethers.

"There's a ball of ice in the pit of my stomach," said Zen to Char at the campfire that night. "Tai-Raynee is so old, after all, isn't it, Char?"

"Yes, Zen. It's hard to argue with so much. It's hard to argue with so many years, so many kors."

"But," Zen looked Char in the eye, "are you saying they can argue with this, what we bring to them? No, Char," said Zen. "They will see it, in the plain light of the day."

Char looked sad. "To them, this world is dark," he finally said. "Maybe too dark for them to see."

The next day, they rode to the fringe of Tai-Raynee, staying close by the forested River Eri. The barbed Cinter rose behind the trees where they camped that night, glowing pale in the night. Clouds boiled gray and purple and green in the sky as an evil broth brewed.

"We will show them our tools and our beasts," Zen said over the fire. "And we will tell them of the great city, and they will see we are right."

"And if they don't, we'll give them a murderous fight," said Kon, staring fiercely at the crimson flames. "They are killers, Zen."

"Yes." Zen looked at Kon. A chilling memory of Win's death flickered in his mind. "But when they will see it with their own eyes the people will stop listening to the sors."

The next morning, they climbed atop the red elks with their weapons and led the tigers and baboons onto the rising plain of Tai-Raynee.

The morning sky oozed with fog and creeping lights. After they had trotted over the gray, misty savanna for a few hours, they encountered a troop of hunters, who ran amazed to meet them.

"Is that Zen?" asked gold Pog, the troop's leader.

"Yes, Pog, it is!" Zen said.

"What is it, then?" gasped gold Pog.

"Beasts we have tamed. We found a great village of stone left behind in that forest, and it is—it's all too much to say now, Pog, but if you love the truth that Hunters have always known, then take your troop with us now. We go to show the sors what we have found."

Pog glanced at the gray Cinter.

Zen followed his eyes and felt the same chill as he saw its cruel point.

"You know the sors, Zen," Pog sighed. "What made you dain you could argue them with Immurtai things? If you knew what they have done..." Pog shook his head.

"Immurtai, *Demurtai*! *Pah!*" Zen scowled. "They've cut us in half, Pog, don't you see? They would make our actions mindless and our minds helpless. Sors have had enough of Eternity. Enough, I say!" Zen's tiger growled and put its paws on Zen's leg. "Don't worry, Tuno," he said, stroking its proud head.

Pog's eyes were wide at the sight of Zen's company. "I could not bear watching such courageous kors go before the sors alone," he said.

And Pog's hunters joined Zen.

Don't Worry, Tuno

They reached the first roads and followed them through the province of the Hunters to the tannery. Hundreds of hunters had already gathered there. Zen shouted from his elk to them.

The sor Tor, sitting beneath the Cinter on his stone block with his brother Turi and two attendants at his side, saw the distant commotion. He whistled to the sor to his right, and soon all the sors were alerted around the circle. They gathered around Tor and looked together at the distant tannery. With a soft gesture, they mustered the Korensis.

"Hunters!" Zen cried. "I have come to tell you we have found a lost world and a better life. I am here to tell the sors about this bright secret, if they will let you hear it. All those who want to hear our tale and support us should come now."

A roar of approval answered from the hunters who stood amazed by Zen's fantastic company. From all directions, kors ran to see Zen and the Immurtians.

They turned on their elks and set off, and the hunters of Tai-Raynee followed.

As they passed through the province of the Hunters, their train increased to thousands. Seeing the growing crowd, kors from other provinces ran out to meet them, waving at the hunters who led the way on the backs of red elks with shining axes in their hands.

As they rode, Zen and the others came upon a sight they could hardly believe.

Rotting in the sun under a swarm of pink flies was a mountain of kors.

As they approached, the limbs and heads of kioros and kioris became visible on the dripping mound. Zen roared, rising in his stirrups. "No! This evil here!" He shook his fist, his eyes wide and rolling like a wolf's. "Away!" He spurred his mount and led his company around the monument, commanding them not to look, yet they all looked, and only Zen's fury overturned their terror.

Char noticed parts of a kor child set on top of the evil mound, and the old hunter wept silent tears of rage for Tai-Raynee as he rode beside Zen.

They passed through the circle of Korensi homes and the innermost circle of crafters, who put down their tools as the Immurtians passed.

Then they came before the Cinter.

On the mound before the cave were the 22 sors. One was seated on a square block of stone. All of their heads were tilted toward the sky. The 5,000 Korensis stood on the hill around them, armed with their tall stone axes.

The Korensis parted, letting Zen and the others ride through on the red elks to meet the sors.

The people of Tai-Raynee pressed behind them as Zen and his fellows drew near the sors and saw the armless and legless sor sitting on the block of stone.

"Sor!" Char hissed.

Zen felt afraid as he looked at the half-kor. "Could it be, Char?"

"I do not know!"

Zen glared at Tor.

Tor was watching a flock of Black Geese far away.

The sors did not look at the tamed red elks, the snarling purple tigers, or the six white baboons, who were baring their fangs at the startled Korensis. White On gestured lightly with his fingerless hand. "Guardians, kill them," he said, softly.

Thunder rumbled from the crowds at Zen's back.

"Will you let us speak?" Zen roared. His elk shifted as the Korensis closed around his company with their spears. The kors pressed forward against the wall of Korensis to hear the sors' answer.

Turi softly jumped from the stone behind his brother and ran toward the cave. The Korensis noticed that he was the High Artist and did not follow him, for they dreaded him.

On's eyes slitted at Zen, surprised. "Your words, I know already, are seduced, corrupted and poisoned. You are spoiled. You are a plague that has come to forget the Truth from Tai-Raynee, to crack its devotion to Forever and to the only Truth, the forever Truth, to the *Koroshi* that continues on like the stars above as kors live and die below. Kill them, so they will reveal the Truth by dying, and by passing away like all the other things, so all may see."

"No, I will be heard!" Zen snapped the leash of Tuno on its haunch and the cat stood erect and snarled proud, its voice echoing off the Cinter.

A gust of awe swept over the kors.

"Tai-Raynee!" Zen shouted. "You see already we have great gifts to offer you. But we have more. We have the magic that makes them possible. We offer you your own hands, your own legs, and your own eyes! We offer you your own world, kors!"

The sors saw the danger building but stayed the Korensis for the moment. Iz spoke: "Tell us what arrogant notion you mean, so your deception may be made plain to all the *Koroshi*. Then we will destroy this evil, as one."

Tor did not look, speak, or even seem to notice the Immurtians.

"You see these things we can do?" Zen asked.

"Whims," Iz said.

"They are real!" Zen frowned, fingering his bow.

"They are false before the Immortals," said white On.

"And so are you," said Zen, "false before the Immortals. And so will all things and kors that will ever exist be false before the Immortals. Or is it these 'Immortals' that are false? You have forgotten where words came from and made them more than what they mean and use them against what they name!"

"You have studied in sin, hunter," gasped Pla.

"Be silent!" said Tor, still staring at the sky. "You are swayed by their words, which are only noises passing like wind," said Tor.

"You have made a breath of air worth more than all who breathe," Zen said. "We have studied only this world and our past," he roared, turning to the crowd. "We have found a great stone village in the forest below the wide lake!"

The kors whispered this news, confused and frightened, as they continued to come to the Cinter from the farthest corners of Tai-Raynee.

"You speak nonsense," said On.

"It is the truth!" cried Zen. "And it is waiting for us all. Kors built a wondrous place long before they came to Tai-Raynee. Hear it now and know it well before it is forgotten again." Zen thrust his brazen axe at the sky. "Know it now and don't forget it, kors!"

White On hissed, waving his fingerless hand.

Holy Tor saw Zen's fantastic claim as his death knell; he closed his eyelids twice at the Korensis.

They struck into the party.

An anguished cry rose from the multitude.

Zen wept as he swung his axe at the attacking Korensis.

The tigers growled and roared in unison, putting the Korensis off for a moment, and in that moment the sky was split with a web of lightning that streaked across the clouded dome in every direction like a cracking bowl of alabaster.

A thunderclap smote the ground.

In the stunned silence immediately after, a terrible, beautiful voice issued from the cave above.

"Tai-Raynee is a grave!"

A chill passed over the kors as the voice rippled over them.

Then Azurel walked out of the cave, with the skull of Holy Sor on her palm and a newborn child in her arm. The High Artist Turi walked beside her.

"Tai-Raynee is your grave, kors!" she cried, and her voice welled in the granite mouth of the cave and reverberated over the plain. "The Cinter is our gravestone!"

Rain fell as two Korensis ran up the hill, sent by Tor.

The guards raised axes at Azurel as they rushed her, but they were afraid to attack for the infant in her arms or for the skull of Holy Sor or for the High Artist who walked beside her. Azurel and Turi walked untouched to the block of stone on which Tor sat as the Korensis wavered before them.

Turi helped Azurel onto the stone of Tor and jumped up after her. He pushed the two attendants off the stone.

"Which one would Holy Tor defend, kors?" cried Azurel, standing before Tor and showing the kors her newborn child and the ancient skull.

Tor gasped.

"Life or death?" asked Azurel.

Tor hissed: "Attack them."

From all sides, the waves of Korensis converged.

The hunters fought back, bitterly, as Rueez spurred his elk up the hill, parting the surprised guards, who were afraid of the bewitched animal.

"Stop!" Turi shouted from behind Tor, holding a knife to his brother's throat.

The Korensis paused.

Rueez spurred his mount and it leaped onto the block of stone.

He lifted Azurel and their child onto the elk.

Azurel threw the skull of Sor onto the stone before Tor and it splintered into shards and dark powder.

A Korensi speared Turi in the back and yet, before he died, he slashed his brother's throat with the knife that created him, finishing his masterpiece.

All the kors leaned forward, as though pulling deep roots from Tai-Raynee, and yet they hesitated before the giant Cinter.

Jak was speared through the throat and fell. The tiger Tuno was stricken down by three spears. The rest were following rapidly as the Korensis closed in around them.

Then the deepest root tore from the soil and all the kors took a step toward the Cinter—a step that became a stampede. Kors hurled themselves against the phalanx of Korensis, each fighting against the Infinite in that desperate moment.

The sky screamed as a vast talon clawed its fabric and spilled through the cloud with a blinding light. The comet streaked into the heavens, wrenching wide the clouds and filling the sky with a fire as bright as a hundred suns.

Kioris and kioros fell on the ground as the fireball passed, hurling over the Cinter and over the northern horizon, and a thunderclap shivered the land when it struck the distant sea.

A spray of orange light spread over the high northern horizon and the earth rumbled beneath them.

The sors were first to rise. "The *Koroshi* has been warned!" called white On, waving his maimed hand at the sky, his voice echoing off the Cinter over the plain.

"Take this warning, O kors!" cried Pla. "We have almost been destroyed by the Truth we tried to defy!"

The kors shivered in cold horror on the fields.

"Heed the omen," commanded Iz.

"Go now, kors, and pray forgiveness," cried white On, waving his fingerless hand.

The kors trembled and wept in broken heaps across Tai-Raynee. The sun shone bright in the suddenly clear sky. The air was strangely still.

One by one, they rose. And together, they turned away.

The sors returned hastily to the cave, carrying the body of Tor.

The sors' guardians finished their work as they struck into the Immurtians.

The sky above was wounded, green and purple.

The great and wild moment had come, and gone away again, forever.

As Zen's brave company fought on, the cave groaned like a beast in pain.

The kors wandering off to their homes turned and looked one last time and saw white foam fill the cave's mouth before a pillar of seawater blast half a stin high into the sky. The kors shrank under the eruption as it climbed, an arch of golden spray glittering with millions of tumbling bones. Ribs and shins and laughing skulls struck the ground in the shining mist, exploding around them on the fields, and the bodies of all 22 sors thudded broken and twisted amid the raining shards.

The bones rained down thick from the sky, darkening the fields, and after the surge abated two more surges blasted into the sky, like eons of burnt offerings to the past unfurling all at once before them.

Then a salt mist lingered over Tai-Raynee. Shattered, limping skull-crabs scrabbled amid the debris and the golden mist swirled through the green sky like a giant, shimmering ghost. The kors stood still as the glowing mist descended, like a great and common spirit, falling softly onto the cheeks of each to join the rivers of their tears.

Rueez and Azurel climbed from their buried dead elk on the mound of bones before the Cinter.

She handed him his daughter, whom they had protected between them from the showering shards.

He took the infant and smiled. He saw his face in hers, and he embraced Azurel, their child between them.

Climbing from his struggling elk, half-buried in skulls, Zen scrambled over the hill of bones toward Azurel and Rueez.

Azurel saw him. "Zen!"

He reached them and she wept and embraced him as she felt and smelled his fur against her again.

Zen looked over Tai-Raynee, fogged with tears and mist. He looked down at a broken skull-crab. Rage and awe and determination entangled his heart.

Azurel tugged his hand and squeezed Rueez's shoulder. She led them both up the slope of skulls and bones that the Cinter had vomited.

They entered the cave. Its walls had been washed clean. They walked over the thick flow of bones to the mantle of rock where the sors had so long presided.

They looked at the niche where the skull of Sor had sat for nine eons.

Beads of seawater dripped over the handsome surfaces of Azurel's statues of kiori, kioro, and child. Somehow they had remained just where she put them when she took the skull of Sor.

Zen put his arms around them then. "Let this be sacred now," he said.

ABOUT THE AUTHOR

New York Times bestselling author Warren Fahy was a bookseller, movie database designer (thousands of his movie descriptions are all over the Internet at different sites like Rotten Tomatoes), helped get a new definition of the word "mullet" into the Oxford English Dictionary and was lead writer for Rock Star Games' Red Dead Revolver. His science thriller FRAGMENT was nominated for a BSFA and an International Thriller Award and is published in 19 languages. The sequel, PANDEMONIUM, is now available along with his epic fantasy, CRIMSON.

BOOK LIST

Fragment
Pandemonium

Crimson
Creating Christ: How Roman Emperors Invented Christianity
The Haunting of Sherlock Holmes and Other Adventures
Magenta
The Kor

CROSSROAD
PRESS

www.ingramcontent.com/pod-product-compliance
Lightning Source LLC
LaVergne TN
LVHW090949080826
845145LV00003B/945